# Bag Limit

## Enough is Never Enough

By

Alana K. Haase

with

Captain Steven F. Gilbert

*I dedicate this story to the many people who spend hours on the water, earning a living, finding peace or both. My heart and compassion go out to the beautiful creatures of the sea whose destiny has been altered by greed or ignorance. And to President Donald Trump, for ending NAFTA.*
*Captain Steven Gilbert*

*Alana would like to dedicate BAG LIMIT to:*
*Matthew Moses Gilbert, the original 'Pea Boy'*

**BAG LIMIT**

**Table of Contents**

# Chapter 1



Artificial reefs are the ultimate in recycling. Large items such as wrecked cars, retired warships, chunks of concrete that have little value on land and will not decompose are cleansed of oil and placed on the ocean floor providing habitat for everything from the smallest invertebrates to the largest predators.

Fish are attracted to the 'reef' as the saltwater dissolves the metal by electrolysis, and the electrolysis sends out a current that the fish are attracted to and follow all the way back to the reef. The reef creates a hydraulic break in the water current that the fish sense and once there, call home. In five and half years the metal is gone and what remains is now a non-artificial reef sustaining all forms of marine life from algae to plankton, barnacles and oysters. The microscopic animals attract small fish like pin and clowns that the snappers love to eat. Groupers enjoy eating snapper, while octopus and sharks love to eat the grouper. So, a home is provided for marine life while a recreational area is provided for divers and most importantly, the dinner bell rings for the ocean's apex predator: the human fisherman.

But while the artificial reefs create places of beauty and wonder, the process of building them is anything but...

Captain 'Matt' Matthew Farrell guided the Reef Runner out of the pass in Destin at 9:30 PM on a hot August night. He was alone headed out into the currently calm seas of the Gulf of Mexico. His deckhand, Charles, was on his way in his 23-foot Mako and would catch him about five to six miles out. Being alone on the Gulf was not a recommended formula for long life, given the unpredictable behavior of Mother Nature and boating in general. Captain Matt was not worried, he had built the Reef Runner himself and had prayed over every one of the two hundred and forty sheets of marine grade ply board, seventeen thousand screws and two hundred and seventy gallons of fiberglass resin that held the fifty foot by twenty-foot vessel together.

The Reef Runner never left her slip without a prayer of blessing and Matt was certain that whatever happened, he and God had it under control.

The moon was full and the silvery light cast diamonds on the calm waters as Matt continued out the pass. This was a peaceful start to his workday, but Matt knew it would not stay that way long. He had two school buses loaded on the front deck to be dropped in the Gulf for artificial reefs for a Charter Captain. The Captain who had commissioned these reefs was a very competitive fisherman who prided himself on out fishing every other charter in Destin. He had commissioned smaller reefs from Matt before and kept the location of these reefs as secret as a moonshine still in the Appalachian Mountains. He was known to have his deckhands shoot bird shot at other charter boats he felt were too close to his fishing spots and kept his numbers in a safety deposit box and his Loran was guarded by a vicious miniature Doberman in his wheelhouse.

Captain Gibson's customers didn't seem to mind the extra excitement as they always came in with record catches of snapper and amberjack to show off. Matt didn't care for the extra pirate drama with Gibby, as he was known to the local fishing community, but he was a good reef customer and like Matt, he loved Destin and the Gulf passionately. His fishing charters were World famous and he brought in a lot of tourist dollars to the small town. Matt laughed, thinking, 'Gibby should change his name to Cook and put mini cannons on the deck!'

Matt continued chuckling picturing Gibby in a pirate costume, fishing with pale tourists all agape at the site as he punched in coordinates of where he was supposed to meet the Captain on his fifty-foot charter vessel, the Lucky Ladyfish, and drop these busses.

He put a baseball cap on his head and radioed Charles, 'Hey man, you coming to work tonight or not? I'm already a mile out the pass.'

Static on the radio did not disguise the fact that Charles had imbibed a few shots of cheap rum.

'Yeah Cap, I'm headed out the harbor now. Catch up in about twenty!'

Matt gave Charles his current coordinates and told him to head due south and hurry up. Two school busses were a heavy load and the drop would be too much for a one-man crew. Charles slurred but assured Matt he was on the way

Matt sighed, a sober deckhand in Destin was rarer than a Baptist church organist playing Amazing Grace in hell. But Charles had spent his entire sun baked life on the Destin harbor and out in the gulf and was as good a deckhand as you could get.

Matt took his hands off the wheel and said a quick prayer and continued into the night.

A drone of engine noise approached, and Matt cut the throttle and turned around. Sure enough, it was Charles in his Mako cutting rooster tails and laughing uproariously. Charles slowed down and got close enough to tie up to the Reef Runner and Matt saw he was not alone.

'Oh no...what has he done now?'

On board the Mako was a tall blonde woman who was having a very hard time standing upright. She was wearing a tiny triangle top bikini that barely covered her nipples, much less her large breasts, cut off blue jean shorts and one shoe. Her bathing suit cover was wrapped around her neck like a scarf and had she been sober she may have been able to untangle it and cover herself. But as she wrestled with the cover while staggering around the front of the Mako laughing like a loon screaming it was obvious the bathing suit cover was not the real problem.

Charles threw a bumper out and tossed Matt a rope. He looked up at Matt and said, 'Sorry Cap, I couldn't leave her alone like this!' He tried to laugh and said, 'You're not mad at me Cap? I'm just trying to help a lady out!'

Matt pointed at the woman who was now sitting on the deck of the Mako still clawing at the bathing suit cover scarf and said, 'I see no 'lady' here...'

'Look man, we have work to do. I cannot do it alone. Now get her on board and get busy. I want you to check the tie downs on the busses and crane. We've got to crank it up and get out to the drop site.'

Charles knew when to shut up. This was one of the reasons Matt put up with him and pushed the drunk woman up the boarding ladder by her butt and scrambled up behind her. Matt checked the lines tying the Mako to the Reef Runner and told Charles to put his 'lady' in the bunkhouse and make her lay down and be quiet. With all lines secure he throttled up to head to the drop site coordinates.

Charles came out of the bunkhouse to check the tie downs but Drunk Barbie, as Matt decided to name her, came right out behind him staggering like a zombie.

'Charles!' Matt yelled from the wheelhouse, 'Get that dang shoe off of her maybe she won't fall and bust her head open if she's barefooted!' Matt knew he was watching his profitable, peaceful night go to Hades in a Handbasket with this nightmare aboard his ship. Charles turned around, grabbed Drunk Barbie around her waist and expertly snatched her one high heeled sandal off her foot and tossed it overboard.

Barbie screamed, 'my shooooooooooeeeeee! Those were expensive you asshole!' She proceeded to start pummeling Charles in his face then when he let go of her waist, she ran away from him to go hide in between the school busses.

Matt was a split second away from completely losing his temper.

As a religious man who was likely the only non-drinking Captain, fisherman, and resident of Destin, Florida this could get serious. Alcohol and the Gulf usually meant trouble and Matt steered clear of it like shallow water.

'Charles!' He yelled, 'Get your woman under control before she falls off the boat! We are ten miles out and if she falls off this boat, she is gonna die!'

They could hear Drunk Barbie wailing about her shoe from somewhere in front of the boat as she thrashed around. Charles had stopped laughing and was looking green around his gills.

'Cap what do you want me to with her? I got the shoe off and I told her dumb ass to lay down? I could tie her up?'

'No No NO!' Matt said, 'Listen to me, do you have any more booze on your boat? If you do make her drink it so she will go ahead and pass out. Put her in the bunk and close the door.'

Charles looked confused, 'Well I have a pint of vodka, but that won't do any good. This chick drinks more than I do!'

Matt sighed. It was decision time...He had never allowed any alcohol consumption on the Reef Runner. Never, ever. It was his covenant deal with God, but this was an exceptional circumstance. Just then there was a loud bang from the front of the boat where Barbie was hiding or looking for sea monsters or her shoe?

'Get it.' Matt commanded. Charles headed to the Mako while Matt set the boat on course and went looking for Barbie.

As Charles came up the ladder with the vodka pint held between his teeth, Matt heard another squeal to his left, a thump and a splash. It could only be one thing; drunk Barbie was overboard in the black waters of the Gulf of Mexico as the clock chimed midnight.

Matt dove toward the edge of the deck where he heard the splash frantically reaching in the dark water.

They say God looks after drunks and little children and by a sure miracle Matt grabbed a handful of blonde hair. He pulled Barbie up and she started screaming loudly enough to call Triton from the depths of Atlantis. She grabbed for Matt's other outstretched hand and sunk her long nails into Matt's arm.

'Charles! CHARLES! Get the damn rope ladder NOW before she pulls me overboard! NOW MAN!' Matt hollered, he did not dare let go of drunk, thrashing screaming Barbie or she would be washed under the boat into the prop, but he was sliding on the deck about to go overboard with her and could not hold on much longer.

Charles appeared at his shoulder and threw the ladder in the water. Laying down on the deck by Matt he managed to tie the ladder to a cleat and brace Matt from being pulled into the drink. Drunk Barbie had now ceased her infernal wailing and was sloshing around at the end of Matt's arms. Matt and Charles managed to wrap her arms on the rope ladder and heaved her up on deck. Barbie laid there in a pitiful mass of blonde hair, wet shorts and her triangle top was now missing. She hiccupped and cried and rolled over so both men had a good view of her expensive boob job.

Matt shook his head and snarled at Charles, 'cover her up and put her in the bunk. I don't care how you do it but make her stay there. Do you understand me?'

Yes Sir, Captain, roger that.'

Charles half carried, half dragged almost passed out, drunk and drowned Barbie to the wheelhouse and took her down to the bunk. He tried to stuff her in a fishing slicker, but he couldn't get her long legs in it and it would not cover her breasts anyway. He wrapped her in a blanket and told her if she got up, he would get fired. She glared at him and was about to say something. Charles said, 'Look, you get me fired I will throw you right back overboard for the sharks to eat you. Understand?'

Barbie halfheartedly murmured some curses and wadded the blanket around her and turned her back on him.

Charles was ready to follow Matt's lead and pray. He knew if she got back up and caused any more trouble, he would never crew the Reef Runner again.

Matt was back at the wheel looking over the deck, taking deep breaths and thanking God that this stupid woman had not drowned or killed him when he saw the pint bottle of vodka Charles had dropped while going for the rope It twinkled like a star in the moonlight laying on the deck behind the busses. His stoh did another flip remembering his covenant deal about booze with God. Matt quickly checked his readings and ran down the deck. He didn't even want to touch the bottle so he kicked it as hard as he could and watched the twinkling bottle slide across the deck and slip over the port side. Matt breathed a sigh of relief, 'Lord, it was an emergency, a one-time thing in an attempt to calm the crazy. No one even drank it.' But to Matt's great dismay he got no reply in his heart.

Matt trudged back to the wheelhouse with his head bowed. Would it do any good to pray the rest of the night would go well? At least they would be at the rendezvous coordinates with Captain Gibby and the Lucky Lady Fish within minutes and this night would soon be over.

Charles reappeared in the wheelhouse. 'Cap I did check all the tie downs; everything is secure and ready.'

'What of your lady friend?' Matt said quietly, 'is she secure? I don't think I need to tell you who is crewing with Captain Gibson tonight, we do not need a topless drunk blonde with huge tits running around the deck when we meet up with them.'

Charles audibly swallowed and said, 'Yes sir, she is wrapped in a blanket and laying down. I think she swallowed a good bit of sea water, so she's passed out. She should stay down there and be quiet.'

Charles took a deep breath and continued, 'Skipper I am sorry, things got bad out of control at ...Well, I'm sorry sir. I will come to the slip tomorrow and clean the boat, tie tires, cut bait or whatever you want me to do. On my time, sir.' He hung his head and waited for Matt's verdict.

Matt stared at Charles with his piercing blue eyes and said nothing. The angrier Charles thought he was would keep him working harder and drinking less. Matt turned his eyes towards the dark horizon, everyone was alive and well and what else could go wrong?

Just then, Matt spotted running lights consistent with a sports fisher and heard Captain Gibson calling on the radio, 'Reef Runner, Reef Runner, Matt is that you?'

The Lucky Lady Fish throttled up and turned towards the starboard side of the Reef Runner to tie up. Allen Cline jumped off the deck of the Lucky Ladyfish onto the Reef Runner with a Bush beer in one hand and a sawed off twelve gauge in the other. He also had beer cans stashed in every pocket available on his jacket. His twin brother Aaron was standing on the deck of the Lucky Ladyfish yelling, 'I'm getting ahead of you asshole!' while waving two more beer cans.

'Whoa Allen? What the Sam Hill do you think you're doing boarding my boat with booze and a gun?' Matt yelled, he may have been a backslider earlier, but his covenant was on his mind. The second time you compromise is easier than the first then you are sunk. 'You know my rules-- get that beer off my boat and point your damn gun at someone else!'  Matt was not surprised at the drunken condition of Gibby's deckhands.

Allen and Aaron Cline were famous for starting the day with beer and they didn't stop till one or the other of the muscular bulldog shaped brothers passed out or took a break to get a new tattoo. They were as strong as oxen and had fished since they could walk and were decent deckhands before the sun went down and too many beers went bottoms up.

Allen had no intention of giving up the gun or the beer. 'Captain Matt I am doing what I was told. You know Capt. Gibby plans on wiping the decks with the competition during the rodeo this year, so this reef is a special secret. I was told to make you turn off your loran and make you follow us to the drop site.'

Beer was running down Allen's chin as he managed to get all these words out in the proper order, so he grinned and took a can emptying gulp. He slapped Matt on the back and said, 'let's go Cap!'

Matt was worn down and just wanted this night over. Back on the Lady Fish Aaron Cline was throwing empty beer cans and howling at the moon. This infuriated the min pin in the wheelhouse who started howling too. Against his better judgment he did not demand Allen throw his beer overboard and turned to the Lady Fish yelled, 'Gibby, I know you can hear me! I am charging you extra for this CRAP. Double and you will pay it!'

He turned towards his own wheelhouse with the twelve gauge between his shoulder blades and Allen spitting beer all over his neck. Matt prickled briefly and thought about turning and snatching the shot gun and whacking Allen right in his fat jaws with it, but the way the night had already gone did he dare chance that it was only loaded with bird shot? Gibby's determination to win the deep sea fishing rodeo come hell or high water had obviously seriously clouded his judgment.

Five miles later, somewhere out in the gulf Matt brought the Reef Runner to a stop behind the Lucky Lady Fish.

Charles ran a rope through the windshield of one of the busses on the front deck of the Reef Runner. He threw the rope over to Aaron who tied it to a cleat on back of the Ladyfish. 'PULL on her Gibby!' he yelled into the radio. Gibby put the throttles on and the bus slid off the deck of the Reef Runner and started to sink into the dark waters.

The Reef Runner and the Lady Fish both throttled back up and moved about five miles away from the first bus and repeated the process of pulling the second bus off the deck into the dark waters.

The seats in the busses were already becoming nesting places for shovel noses lobsters as barnacles and oysters began to encrust the bus and snapper and grouper began happily swimming in and out of the windows of their new home.

Now that the reefs were dropped, Allen who had become quite sullen with his brother eight beers ahead of him dropped the twelve gauge. It hit the deck and went off with an explosion shooting a large hole in Matt's wheelhouse.

Allen screamed as he and Charles hit the deck. Matt dove for the gun and scooped it up and ejected the spent shell. The gun was fully loaded, and Matt calmly unloaded the gun and threw the shells overboard. He went to the starboard side and waited.

Captain Jeff 'Gibby' Gibson came out of his wheelhouse and finally faced Matt.

'Matt! We've been friend's forever dude! You know he didn't mean to! This is business, I need these reefs to remain quiet!'

'Jeff, you and your crew have been drinking since ten am. Get your gunslinger back on your ship of fools and know that I'm sending you a bill for the fiberglass repairs. You will pay for my material, time and downtime charges for my boat while it's under repair. You will also pay double for the busses. If this bill is not paid in full by five PM, I will be at the Captains table at AJ's to tell everyone there exactly how the Reef Runner got holes shot in the wheelhouse tonight and where we were and what we were doing when it happened. We clear?'

Captain Jeff Gibson faced Captain Matthew Farrell eye to eye, boat to boat, man to man. Gibby knew that despite tonight shenanigans Matt could find his way back to his wonderful new reef if he wanted to and he was paying for silence so he could win the rodeo.

He nodded. 'you got it Matt, 'appreciate you man.'

Matt nodded back and said, 'get your deckhand off my boat.'

Jeff waved his arm at Allen, 'Get over here and let's be done now.

Hey Matt! You can keep the gun too, we have more!' Aaron was too drunk and having a hard time walking the deck of the Lady Fish to help his brother get back aboard. Allen who had scrambled to his feet and checked himself for a gunshot wound sauntered over to the rail and prepared to jump on the stern gunwale of the Lady Fish but could not resist a parting shot at Matt. He turned and yelled, 'Nice holding you up tonight Cap Matt!' He jumped and with his beer impaired state and white fishing boots he slipped and fell back onto the deck of the Reef Runner whacking his head so hard Matt expected brains to be scattered on his deck like scrambled eggs.

'Are you kidding me?' he thought, 'can it get any worse?'

Just then a wave rocked the tied-up boats and Allen slid right off the bow into the water under the Reef Runner.

'SHIT! Grab him!' Jeff was screaming and laughing.

Matt just knew he was about to wake up. In his nice warm bed, next to his nice warm wife and tell Donna what a horrible dream he had, but right then all he could do was find something, anything to save this newest drunken fool who fell off his boat tonight.

Matt sprinted to the wheelhouse and all he could find was an empty bleach bottle and some dock line. Where was Charles? Where was the rope ladder?

Matt tied the bottle to the line and tossed it to Allen who had resurfaced and was flapping his arms while trying to get out of his jacket and white rubber boots. Allen grabbed the bottle and to his credit, thought Matt, for someone who had been drinking for at least seventeen hours was immediately able to calm down and follow instructions. Matt towed him around to the starboard side of the boat where the rope ladder was still tied. Allen managed to crawl up on his own and get on deck. Unlike drunken Barbie, Matt noted, Allen didn't lose a boot or his jacket.

Over on the Lady Fish, Gibby was laughing uproariously about Allen almost dying. 'Ok boys, enough fun! Allen get on this damn boat right now and let's all go home. Matt, I'll see you tomorrow my man! Good work!'

Matt didn't bother reply, he was emotionally spent and looked at Allen and waved towards the bow and turned his back.

There was no further yelling or howling from Aaron and Matt assumed he had passed out on deck and missed almost losing his twin. Allen's swim in the gulf had sobered him up quite a bit and he reached out to pat Matt on the shoulder. 'Dude, I'm sorry. Thanks....'

Matt grabbed the collar of Allen's jacket and twisted him around. 'Dude? I am the Captain of this ship and don't you ever forget it or address me as dude.  Your Captain told you to get off my boat. Now get off my boat and try not to kill yourself this time.'

Back in the wheelhouse, Matt for the second time tonight had to take deep breaths and say a prayer of thanks that no one died. But before he could even say, 'amen' the though popped up. Where is Charles?

Charles had secured the crane after dropping the busses and was curled up in the bunk with drunk Barbie, both passed out cold.

The Lucky Lady Fish was long gone, and Matt fired up the Reef Runner and headed back to Destin.

Sometime close to five AM Matt was back at his house on a quiet neighborhood cull de sac.

He slipped inside silently and made his rounds. In the first bedroom was a set of bunk beds. In each bunk was a head of blonde curls so like his own, on his six-year-old twin boys. Joshua and Caleb. Matt stood there for a moment, admiring his son's and the perfect peace they slept in.

The next bedroom was a pink palace that contained his princess. Like her older brother's three-year-old Abigail slept in perfect peace surrounded by her outrageous collection of stuffed animals. Tonight's favorite was her pink dolphin, Flipper. Flipper had outranked the bears, lambs and dolls to ride the pillow with Abby tonight.

Last Matt headed to his own bedroom. His wife, Donna, was sleeping as peacefully as the children, sprawled out over her pillows and most of Matt's too. Matt brushed a lock of auburn hair off her face and she smiled and rolled over but did not awaken.

Matt headed to the bathroom and quietly shut the door. He knew the kids would wake up in about an hour and Donna would have her hands full for the day. He turned on the shower and stepped in to rinse the sea salt from his mind and his body as he wondered, 'was this worth it?

The hours spent researching reefs, materials, ship building, permits, coast guard inspections, more permits, more research, fishing and dealing with crazy people, drunk people and worse the Coast Guard?

The warm water hit his tanned and muscled body and the wondering went down the drain with the saltwater. 'yes, it's worth it' he thought. To Matt, his title of 'father' meant 'provider' and he was providing, and Donna got to be a stay at home mom, baseball mom, classroom mom, Sunday school teacher and God only knew what else she took on in the community. Father's provide, mom's nurture so at the end of the cull de sac his family had it all. And Matt knew that what he was doing was good for the environment, providing clean habitats, keeping the oceans healthy while providing a good living for multiple areas of commerce including dive shops, snorkel boats and those fish crazy fisherman who drink too much.

But it was worth it.

# Chapter 2

*AUSTIN, TEXAS*

Theodore John Hollis the Third stared up Congress Avenue at the Texas State Capitol building. The pink granite glowed in the setting sun of Texas and Ted felt a tug at his heart. He wanted to crawl to the top of this huge building and kiss the Goddess of Liberty square in her ugly mug. He wanted to own her and take her Lone Star back to his house and mount it on his front door. He laughed at the thought, 'I am a native son.' He smiled and straightened out his red silk tie. Even the light silk was suffocating in the Texas heat.

Ted walked down Congress Avenue and ducked into the Austin Hotel. He strolled through the lobby and headed to the bar. 'Teddy! Join us son!' a gravelly voice called out from a dark booth. It was his grandfather, Theodore Abraham Hollis, holding court with three other suits and a lovely blonde cocktail waitress who smiled at Ted.

Ted smiled at the waitress, 'Now if you don't want me calling you Papaw in public don't call me Teddy!' He laughed and bent to hug the old man.

Theodore Abraham roared with laughter and smacked the blonde on her round bottom. 'Bring my grandson a whiskey and a Cuban darlin' and hurry up about it! I like the way you wiggle when you hurry!'

The other suits laughed at the elder Theodore's comment and stood to greet his grandson. 'Please call me Ted.' Ted said as he shook hands with Andrew Armstrong and Boyd Croft. He remembered meeting these men before. Flipping through the rolodex in his brain he nailed them: Armstrong was a Congressman from Mississippi and Croft was a well-known corporate tax attorney from San Antonio. He held no allegiance to any particular corporation and was rumored to be worth more than he charged which was a tremendous amount.

The third man did not stand but remained seated beside Ted's grandfather watching Ted intensely through bright green eyes. Ted turned to him and the man extended his hand, 'Senator Alexander Thibodaux,' Ted said,' I believe we met briefly at my father's home last Christmas sir.' 'You have a good eye for people son. That skill will take you far in this business, hone it.' Replied the United States Senator from Louisiana.

Ted looked at the older man and took in his Zegna suit with appreciation. 'Call me Alex and I'll call you Ted. The way your grandfather has been bragging on your business skills I can't bring myself to call you Teddy Boy.' The senator didn't miss the younger man's assessment and admiration of his suit, custom made shirt or his eye's lingering on his platinum Rolex Daytona.

The waitress reappeared with Maker's Mark served neat and water backs for all five men. 'Mr. Hollis, the concierge is on the way with a humidor to offer you a selection of fine cigars from Cuba, The Canary Islands and Cameroon.'

'Hot damn! You're a fine little filly! That sounds wonderful and now I'm going to pay you just to walk back and forth of this here booth so I can watch!' The elder Hollis laughed uproariously at his own hilarity and slapped the table.

Ted paid no attention to his grandfather's antics. He was taking stock of everyone at this meeting and trying to put together the reason for this meeting with these players. His father and grandfather were letting him in on more of the family's business holdings and Ted was hungry for a bigger piece of the Hollis pie. And if he couldn't have his father's senate seat in Washington then by God and Texas he would go for the Governor's Mansion in Austin.

'That little blonde gal is as cute as a speckled pup, ain't she Alexander?' Theodore Abraham jabbed the Louisiana Senator in the ribs and laughed. The blonde threw both men an award-winning smile and a wink as she sashayed by the booth.

Maker's flowed and cigars were selected with an appropriate nod from the cigar concierge.

Ted sipped his bourbon and leaned into the table. He had trained himself to listen to several conversations at once and he tuned into the Mississippi Congressman discussing tariffs and profit margins with the tax attorney. His grandfather and the Louisiana Senator were discussing the language of the new trade agreement with Canada and Mexico called NAFTA. The tax attorney joined in and added that NAFTA was going to allow for some very interesting international personal business investment. All four men smiled.

The concierge returned to the booth and announced that the maître' d and the chef were ready in the private dining room as soon as the gentlemen were.

In the private dining room, the men sat down in a flurry of suit jackets and lingering cigar smoke. Theodore Abraham removed his suit jacket and was yanking at his already loosened tie. He pulled the $300 bluebonnet blue swatch of silk out of his collar and tossed it to Ted. 'Here son, this damn thing is choking me, and I don't need that while chewing my cud.' Ted sat down by his grandfather at the round table and neatly folded the expensive tie. His grandfather gave the impression of having no appreciation for fine things, but Ted knew this was not true as he gently placed the folded silk into his grandfather's jacket pocket for safekeeping.

A gigantic black man in a tuxedo approached the table followed by the blonde cocktail waitress bearing a tray of ice waters.

'Ah Caesar, good to see you my man' Hollered Abraham. Caesar smiled and bowed slightly, 'Mr. Hollis, it is always a pleasure sir.'

His melodious voice was quietly soothing, and he place a tumbler of ice and a bottle of spring water by each man's plate.

'What will be your pleasure tonight, sir?'

'You know what I want! Get me a big steak, wipe it's ass, smack it's butt across the grill and bring it on in here, I'm starved!'

Caesar smiled; his white teeth looked like piano keys in his large mouth. 'Mr. Hollis will enjoy the 16 oz ribeye, rare to medium rare with a twice baked potato smothered in bacon and sharp cheddar. Very good sir!'

Caesar continued to Abraham's left, Boyd Croft looked at Caesar over his menu and said, 'Blackened redfish with grilled asparagus.'

Ted looked up in surprise, 'who comes to the heart of Texas cattle country and orders fish?' he thought.

Then Armstrong handed his menu to Caesar and smiled, 'Blackened redfish here too, but I want the loaded potato.' Armstrong keep smiling and looked at Ted and said, 'redfish put more money in my pocket and cows are plentiful in Mississippi too.'

Ted glanced down at his menu again, he wanted to avoid eye contact and think. 'they are sending a message. What is it?'

Alexander Thibodaux had been watching Ted throughout the ordering process and he leaned back and smiled too. He didn't even glance at Caesar but said, 'Well boys, one fish won't break the bank. I'm back in Washington in the AM and there's plenty of fish in that sea. I'm going to join Hollis and have a fillet.'

Caesar chimed in, 'Senator Thibodeau will have an 8 oz fillet mignon, medium rare with lightly steamed asparagus and drawn butter on the side.'

Caesar looked at Ted and he realized all eyes were on him Ted was like his father and grandfather before him, he was raised on fine Texas beef and nothing pleased him more than a perfectly grilled steak. The steaks here were legendary, even in Texas and he sure hated not to have one but something fishy was going on at this table.

Ted took a deep breath and informed the men and Caesar, 'Well there is a federal ban on red fish and snapper in Louisiana which should make Senator Thibodeau unhappy but makes Congressman Armstrong very happy. This fish either swam in from Mexico or was farmed in Mississippi to fuel the Cajun cooking fad I've heard so much about. This piece of fish has the value of fine Texas beef according to this menu so I will give a try as well. Blackened please, Caesar with the potato'

Caesar smiled and bowed again as he collected the last menu from Ted. 'I will place the gentlemen's order at once with the chef.'

Abraham chuckled deeply and clapped Ted on his shoulder, 'Good choice my boy, I'm proud of you. Not only are you bankrolling the Congressman's fishing business but checking out the price tag shows your appreciation of the laws of supply and demand and your granddaddy's wallet!'

Ted glanced over at the Congressman and Senator. Alex smiled and shrugged, 'Ted my business interests are vast and not confined to the state of my birth, or even the country of my origin. I have no problem helping out my friends, especially if a piece of the pie is available to me.'

He continued, 'It was a coon ass from Opelousas who started a nationwide craze for our fish. God bless him, the resulting ban served to protect our recreational fisherman who spend a lot of money fishing in gulf waters. A few old commercial fishermen who don't even pay the equivalent in taxes of what a sports fishing yacht may spend in a weekend is acceptable collateral damage. Plus, the increased demand has opened new investment opportunities for Armstrong and further south as well. The Gulf of Mexico Fishery Management Council has been very helpful in increasing conservation in the gulf as have our friends in Washington.'

Ted glanced down as Caesar returned with house salads for all five men. He then faced Thibodaux and said, 'The NAFTA agreement will greatly increase profits from Mexico's imports due to decreased trade tariff's as well.'

'Indeed, it will son, indeed it will.' The Senator said with a smile, 'Mexico has zero bag limits or restrictions on species and Mexican deckhands work very cheap.'

'I head back to Washington to see to the final details before the signing then I would like to come home and do some fishing myself. You are more than welcome to join me and see about your grandfather's latest investment vehicle. I can't seem to convince him to come himself. He's afraid of water!'

Ted started to laugh, and his grandfather slammed his hand on the table, making the water goblets jump again. 'Damn it, Alex, I don't care how big the boat is, if it does not have a casino and cute waitress's I'm not going out there with you!'

'Well send your grandson, he's the perfect choice.'

Ted took another glance at the Senators gleaming Rolex and did not bother to wait for his grandfather's shouted approval. He picked up his water goblet and extended it to the Senator, 'I'll be there sir!'

All five men chuckled and toasted as Caesar reappeared with sizzling steaks and slabs of seared fish covered in aromatic spices and butter.

# Chapter 3



Matt got up at 11:30 and stopped at Destin Elementary School on his way to the docks. He got his visitor pass at the front desk and headed to the lunchroom where he intercepted two blonde boys in the lunch line. 'Daddy!' screamed Joshua and Caleb squeezing Matt from each side. Matt laughed and told them to get their lunch and go sit at the parents table. He left them in line and stopped by the teachers table and kissed Donna.

'Hey hon! Did you rest?' Donna didn't even wait for an answer as she went on, 'Do you mind if I eat here? We are planning the little league party and picking out the trophies.'

Matt smiled and nodded at the teachers, 'No problem, I just wanted to see the boys I don't have a trip tonight, just some boat repairs this afternoon.'

'Oh good!' said Donna, 'if you're just going to be at the docks today can you bring home some shrimp for dinner?' The teachers all oohed and aahed one joined in, 'I'll buy if you fry!'

Matt laughed and said, 'Not a problem my love, do you want jumbos to fry or are you making gumbo?'

'Get mediums to fry please, you know Abby gets upset when the shrimp are bigger than her mouth.' Donna turned to the teacher who spoke up and invited her to come over and eat while handing Matt a paper bag, 'Later babe!'

Matt took the lunch sack and gave Donna's ponytail a playful tug. He headed over to the parents table and was glad to see no other parents sitting down. He was tired after the long crazy night and only a 4-hour nap. He just wanted to hang out with his boys and talk about baseball, fishing or nothing.

The boys were more interested in what kind of cake was going to be served and if they may be awarded a trophy than baseball stats and they were content that their dad was a good listener today. At the bell they jumped up and got back in line waving bye to Matt as he saw them out of the lunchroom.

Matt drove south to the docks envisioning the school busses sending out the invisible homing signal and fish coming from miles around, happy to have a home at last.

He walked down the dock and saw Charles, puking over the side of the Reef Runner as he cut bait. Charles had squid and putrid gut all over the cutting board and in between heaving was placing the cut squid in buckets.

'Charles! We don't have a fishing trip till this weekend, what are you doing?'

Charles looked up in embarrassment and surprise. 'Hey Cap, well... I was just going to get all this ready by the time you got here, you know. Because...Well I just wanted to have it all done for you.'

'Man, we don't fish till this weekend. Just put what you've got cut in containers in the freezer, but I do need you this weekend for that trip and we'll need a ton of fresh bait before the guests get here? Ok? Right now, get a grip and help me repair the damage to the wheelhouse.'

'ten-four Cap!' Charles was very enthusiastic to stop cutting stinky bait during his colossal hangover. He quickly knocked squid guts overboard and put lids on his buckets to contain the fragrance and hosed the deck and cutting boards off.

Once he got done cleaning up, Charles dry heaved one more time and headed towards the wheelhouse. Matt was writing measurements on a notepad.

'Charles I'm going to replace the entire wall. With the shotgun holes it will look terrible if we just patch it. Can you go get me a sheet of marine grade? I wrote the measurements down here and I need some gelcoat. I have glass and resin. You go get this for me while I take the wall down and we will replace it once you get back.'

Charles grabbed the paper and took off. He would have to go right by AJ's to get to the Marine Supply Depo and could run in and grab a shot of rum. Medicinal rum, for his hangover. He felt better already as he ran down the dock.

When Charles returned to the Reef Runner after three shots a beer and getting the plywood, Matt had already removed the shot-up wall and sanded the edges to prep the new wall. He was standing at the front of the boat talking to one of the local junk yard men. Matt had a good relationship with all the local junk yard owners in the panhandle area. They were his source for all the wrecked cars, old tires and other reef building materials.

Ricky the Wrecker Man had just dropped six cars on front of the Reef Runner.

Charles heart sank, he had left his tab open at AJ's and told his favorite bartender he would be right back. 'Cap? I got the wood, but I thought you said we didn't have a trip tonight?'

Matt turned around and looked at Charles waving his hand at the wood, 'Put that by the wheelhouse, I got everything ready. And we don't, these cars will go out tomorrow night.'

Matt turned to Ricky and shook his hand. 'I'll come by and see what else you I have can use. I have two more orders for large ones. If you get anymore school busses, I need you to save them for me.'

'Will do Captain, give us a call by the end of the week. If we don't get any busses in, I can call upstate.'

Ricky left and Matt called to Charles, they used tie downs to secure the crashed and trashed cars to the deck for safekeeping.

Matt and Charles headed back to the wheelhouse and laid the fiberglass on the wood for the new wheelhouse wall. 'Roll the resin on smoothly Charles, good fiberglass has no bubbles in it.'

Charles enjoyed the chemical smell of the resin far more than the stench of squid, so he followed his instructions to the letter. He had a nice buzz going from his medicinal rum and the fiberglass resin when he looked up and saw two Coast Guard crewmen standing on the dock looking at the Reef Runner.

'Captain?' he said, pointing at the men.

Matt looked up, 'What are they looking at?'

'The cars Cap.'

'Roll this smooth and let it set. Rinse that roller in the acetone as soon as you are done.' Matt headed towards the bow towards the men on the dock. 'Help you?' He yelled.

'Permission to board?' said one of the men.

'Come ahead' replied Matt.

'You Captain Matthew Farrell?'

'Yes I am.'

'These the cars you are using to make artificial reefs?'

'Why?'

'They are not crushed; you can't use them if they are not crushed.'

'What do you mean they are not crushed?'

'Captain, you know what I mean. They must be crushed flat. You can't take these cars out there.'

Matt sighed; these guys were getting on his last nerve already. 'Crushed, SIR, according to Webster's dictionary is anything other than original shape due to impact. Every one of these cars has been wrecked and I take a sledgehammer to them and dent them down even more. They are crushed as far as I'm concerned.'

Mr. Coast Guard crossed his arms over his chest and puffed up. 'No Captain, they have to be crushed flat. Like going down the road on a truck flat.' Matt crossed his arms and faced the officer. 'What is the measurement?'

'What do you mean, the measurement?' said Mr. Coast Guard. He was starting to look very annoyed behind his Ray Ban's.

Matt said, 'If I'm at 32 inches is that legal? Or is it 28 inches?'

Coast Guard interrupted and threw up a hand, 'I don't know the measurement!'

Matt continued, 'then you don't have a law to enforce here. If there was an actual law, you would have exact dimensions stating what measurement these cars must be crushed to. So, this is just some idea that someone sitting behind a desk somewhere gave you to keep me from building a reef. Now you need to come back to me with a state statute, voted on and approved by the state of Florida. Then you will have an actual law to enforce. I'm not surrendering or giving in to you.'

Mr. Coast Guard's mouth was hanging open. He looked like a fish out of water and in uniform. Matt smiled at him.

'Now sir, I do happen to have an extra copy of the 1985 National Artificial Reef Plan on my desk. I can get you a copy if you need one. It's the technical memorandum from NOAA with appendices from the US Army Corp of Engineers, your very own fine branch of service and the National Fishing Enhancement Act of 1984. I may not be Japanese, but I am contributing to the enhancement of the fishery management techniques in an environmentally friendly and cost-efficient way by using scrap material as indicated in the manual.'

Matt stood there and continued to smile. Mr. Coast Guard snapped his mouth shut, opened it and snapped it shut again. He opened his mouth one more time and said, 'Well... Very good Captain, see that you continue to do that.'

He stomped off the Reef Runner and Matt took a deep breath. He walked back to where Charles was still sniffing resin by the wheelhouse. Charles took a deep breath too. 'Cap, I sure am glad you actually read all those books and regulations and stuff. Makes me feel safe working for you with those guys snooping around.'

Matt sighed again, 'Charles, I wish those guys would get their rules and regulations straight. Ideas are not enforceable, it's not a law! I've got permission to build reefs and until the man who issued my legal permit to do so revokes it and says I no longer have permission or a permit I'm going to haul reefs! I've got a family to feed and bills to pay.'

Matt shook his head, 'The Japanese have spent, no invested, billions of dollars in their artificial reef programs and have increased seafood production to feed all those people over there because of it. All we are doing is taking scrap that would clog up a landfill and doing the same thing to benefit our economy. We turn junk into food! Good food! Those guys put their pants on one leg at a time just like I do. I don't understand why they act this way...'

Matt took another deep breath. Speaking of food, he had promised Donna fresh shrimp for dinner. He instructed Charles to apply gel coat over the dry resin and roll it smooth and he was done for the day. He told him to be back tomorrow evening to haul these cars and reminded him of the fishing charter for the weekend. Charles bobbed his head in agreement and got a bucket of gel coat and a fresh roller.

Matt surveyed the wheelhouse, decided it was good and told Charles he would see him tomorrow. He jumped off the Reef Runner and took one more look back at the cars on deck and Charles rolling gel coat and headed down the dock.

Matt walked slowly, looking what boats were back in that may have been out fishing today. Captain Butch of the Bushwhacker was back in from a commercial trip. He owed Matt for a reef and probably had fresh fish aboard. If he had just come in and sold his catch this was prime time for Matt to catch him for payment on the reef.

Matt walked towards the Bushwhacker's slip and saw Alfred Hinson. Alfred had deck handed for Matt too when Charles was unavailable due to intoxication. Alfred was washing the boat.

'Hey Alfred! Where's Butch?'

Alfred looked up and waved a deck brush at Matt. 'Hey Cap! Captain Butch is up the fish house. He told me to wash the boat and he'll pay me for the trip when he gets back.' Matt smiled; this was standard operating procedure in Destin. If the Captain paid the deckhands before the boat got washed, the boat did not get washed. Matt told Albert he would be back to see Butch and headed towards the Dock Café' for a coffee.

Several captains were at the dock and the hot topic was the snapper regulations. The captains were complaining that they just could not make a living with these regulations. Why would you regulate the snapper and tell people you couldn't catch them when you were out fishing and couldn't catch anything but a snapper? Most boats were throwing back anywhere from 60-80 snapper a day! All this did was provide free meals for the dolphins in the area. After two years of this nonsense all the dolphins did was chase charter boats looking for free food.

The gulf's once proud, apex predator, reduced to annoying beggars. None of the captains had any idea what to do with these regulations but all were unanimous that this was a dumb ass idea courtesy of the Marine Fisheries Commission. The complaining continued as the captains swore you couldn't make a down without catching a snapper and had anyone at the Marine Fisheries ever been fishing in the gulf? Who was giving them the fish populations numbers?

One captain suggested that the genius's at Sea World would crack dolphin speak and admit to the authorities that the local Flipper's were loving the free Happy Meals in Destin. Another captain spilled his coffee as he waved his hands around yelling, 'we can't keep the damn fish, but we throw them back and a damn dolphin eats it and we are in violation of the damn Marine Mammal Protection Act! You can't feed wild dolphin! Let the damn Coast Guard catch you doing that shit!'

Matt handed this captain a pile of napkins to wipe up his coffee and left the café'. The captain's angry words followed him back to the Bushwhacker. 'Damned if you do, Damned if you don't.'

Matt walked up to the Bushwhacker and the drama continued as Captain Butch was seriously hot under the collar and screaming at Alfred. It appeared that Alfred had broken out a can of white paint and had a four-inch brush in his hand. He had been smacking white paint on the back of the boat.

Matt said, 'Hey Skipper, what is going on? Alfred what are you doing?'

Alfred Gibson was a good deckhand, but it was rumored his suffered from PTSD after his stint in Vietnam. He pointed the brush at Butch and told Matt, 'I don't think the former president wants 'Wacker' besides his name!'

Matt just stood there scratching his head, he had no words for Captain Butch or Alfred. Butch was fuming. The back of his boat had been badly painted white and instead of the Bushwhacker his charter boat was now the Bush.

Matt pulled Butch aside and got paid for the reef then beat a quick exit. He managed not to smile until he was out of earshot of Butch then bent over roaring laughter. Just another insane day in Destin!

Cash in hand, Matt went looking for medium shrimp so he could go home.

# Chapter 4



*SOMEWHERE OFF THE COAST OF LOUISIANA*

Ted Hollis arrived in New Orleans in his grandfather's Gulfstream. He was looking forward to seeing Senator Thibodaux again now that the NAFTA trade agreement had been officially signed. He wanted to take back a blank check of knowledge and present it to his father and grandfather. Senator Thibodaux had been at the new president's side for the signing of this historic bill with a huge smile on his face.

A Cadillac Escalade was waiting at the private runway to take Ted to meet the senator. The senator had let Ted know that the weekend trip would take place at the New Orleans Big Fish and Game Club which was sponsoring a bill fishing tournament. These high-end tournaments have huge cash prizes that bring in elite sportfishing teams from all over the world. Ted slipped into the cool vehicle grateful for air conditioning in the stifling New Orleans humidity.

The escalade wove through the nightmare of New Orleans traffic and arrived at the Yacht Club in about fifty-five minutes. Ted got out and was greeted by a young oriental man with a crew cut dressed in spotless white shorts and a yacht club t-shirt. He spoke perfect English with a southern and far eastern twang.

'Senator Hollis, good to meet you sir, my name is Adam, The Captain and Senator Thibodaux is waiting for you on board.' The young man put Ted's bag in the back of a golf cart, and they drove down to the marina.

The marina was buzzing with activity and every slip was filled with sportfishing or luxury pleasure yachts. Ted took in the material wealth so flagrantly displayed with a deep appreciation. He wished his father and grandfather were more interested in this mode of transportation and recreation. Crews scurried up and down the dock with carts full of expensive luggage and even more expensive fishing gear. The young man turned right down a dock. Ted was gawking at a colossal luxury yacht that took up the entire end of the dock at the bayside. It was 110 feet long with a shining black hull and crew members scrubbing the decks in preparation for the owners. NO LIMITS was its name outlined in neon lights behind the flybridge. With a full- time Captain and a crew of four, this baby easily cost a cool half million a year just to keep her going. Ted was so busy admiring this trophy of capitalism he did not realize that they had stopped at the slip beside the No Limits.

Ted found himself boarding a G&S sportfishing yacht, the Reel Good, with Senator Thibodaux already aboard and waiting on him on the back deck with an open bar and smoldering cigar.

'Ted! So glad you could make the trip. I swear I have never understood your grandfather's aversion to boats. Your father does not share that does he?'

Ted shook the senator's hand, 'No sir, it's just as Texan's we are a land loving sort and Granddad is the Texas Land Commissioner! But I could get very used to this. Thanks for the invite, I have been looking forward to this more than you know.'

'I think it will be a very rewarding trip for us both, son. Fix yourself a drink, the bar has anything you want from sweet tea to scotch. Whatever you are thirsty for.'

Ted's eyes shot another appreciative glance at the No Limits. 'Yes sir, thank you.' He grabbed an ice-cold water bottle and sat down beside Alexander.

'So, we are fishing in a tournament this weekend?'

'That's the deal son, the entry fee is paid for The New Orleans Big Fish and Game Club on this vessel so we can catch a sea monster and win some money! Whatever we want to do, fish till we drop!'

A blonde man in his mid-forties came down from the bridge to join the two men on deck. He extended a muscular tanned arm to Ted. 'Welcome aboard the Reel Good, I'm Captain Brad Fisher. Any friend of the senator is a friend of mine, just let me or the hand know. His name is Adam and he's stowing your bag in your berth below.'

'Thanks, it's good to meet you too, are you a tournament fisherman?'

Brad ran his hands through sun streaked hair that looked like he never combed it and didn't have to, his tan was year-round, and his eyes sparkled as blue as the gulf waters. 'Yes, I am, this is my little boat here, I was lucky to be backed by the senator several years ago in a tourney so I could bankroll this operation and do what I love for a living. I fish tourney's and do charter's full time so anytime the Senator needs some aquatic R and R I am happy to oblige.

My home port is Destin, but I fish all over the gulf, the east coast and Caribbean as well. The Bahama's hosts four big billfish tournaments and we won two of them last year.'

Destin, Florida?' questioned Ted.

'Yeah man, you know it. The worlds luckiest drinking village with a fishing problem?' Brad laughed a deep belly laugh, 'or something like that. I think that is what the tourist board came up with. Historically it's just a fishing village but the beaches are so beautiful it's a big tourist spot now.'

'My wife and I spent a vacation there; she loved the beaches and that soft white sand. But she complained about the shopping the entire week!'

'Shopping? Well that is a woman for you.' Laughed Brad, 'You should have hired me and gone fishing. The ladies do good fishing and most of them actually enjoy it.'

Ted laughed and smiled at Brad and the Senator. 'Well I can't see Mellie enjoying fishing over shopping, but she would probably try it one time. I'll keep that in mind.'

'Well my man, here is the thing, if they don't like it, they will never bother you again about going. If they do like it, you get to go fishing all the time. You just have to take her too, it's a win-win! Get her away from that mall!'

The three men laughed, and Adam showed up from below deck with a cheese tray and set it down.

Senator Thibodaux spoke up, 'Brad we are just waiting on Michael Brandon is that right?' He stabbed a slice of cheese with a frilly toothpick.

'Yes sir,' replied Brad, 'he told me a business associate from Tampa was coming in too, but I think he canceled. So, we are just waiting on Michael. He's probably stuck in traffic.'

Brad turned to Ted and said, 'Michael is a famous New Orleans chef, but he realized that the big money was not in selling po boy sandwiches but bringing in the fish for other restaurants. He has a fish company and opened a market that is bringing in the gold. Now his genius was the restaurant. It's like a Cajun fishing shack beside the market, the food is amazing, the atmosphere is terrible, and the tourists just eat it up. Michael does all kinds of cooking shows and sells stuff. Between the shows, cookbooks, pots and pans, spices and all the other crap he has slapped his name and mug on he is doing pretty good. Might buy his own yacht and quit bothering me! But the big bucks are in the water right now.' Brad looked out into the bay and got quiet.

Ted's instincts told him that this man was the ticket to the investment opportunity the Senator had alluded to for him and anxiously turned towards the dock to see if anyone was coming.

'Adam!' The young deck hand scurried up from belowdecks. 'Yes Captain?'

'Go check the clubhouse and see if Michael Brandon is up there hawking spices or signing autographs!'

'Yes sir!' The young skinny man hopped over rail onto the dock and took off in the golf cart towards the marina.

'So, Brad, you live in Destin but fish here as well?'

'Yeah, that is how it works.' Brad replied. 'My home port and full-time slip is in Destin. I do charters out of Destin and anywhere else someone wants to go. I follow the tournaments for my own pleasure and bank. The truth is the gulf is my home. That makes me a citizen of Texas, Louisiana, Mississippi, Alabama and Florida!' He grinned, looking out at the shimmering water again. 'It's a good life. I enjoy it. Plus, when I show up at these tourney's the local's tremble!' He let out a deep belly laugh, 'Destin fisherman are feared and revered my friend! We fish to win! Destin fisherman hold many world records on everything from the bills to grouper. You think I'm kidding or bragging? Check the Bahama's, it's a Destin boy who places 1st or 2nd every tourney. They hate us man! It's awesome!'

'Bonjour! Salut!' came a yell from the dock. Adam was driving the golf cart and beside him waving a silver can was a large laughing man. He resembled a Buddha with a dark beard wearing a Panama Hat. As rotund as he was tall, he hopped out of the golf cart before Adam had even stopped and was aboard the Reel Good as gracefully as a ballet dancer.

'Ca va?' he yelled, waving his beer can and laughing, 'Joie de vie! Let's go have some fun boys!' he plopped his girth on a deck chair beside Ted. 'Howdy Texan, I'm Michael.'

His laughter was infectious, and Ted could not help chuckling as he introduced himself.

'Oh, I know your folks, your mother is a friend of mine and very good customer. I hope she has managed to teach her housekeeper how to care for cast iron skillets by now. But it wouldn't hurt my feelings if she needs to buy a new set!'

Teddy laughed along with Michael. He remembered his mother had purchased an entirely new kitchen with all the goodies after taking a Cajun cooking class she attended with other senator's wives. His mother was now convinced that the way to cook fine Texas beef was to sear it in cast iron. These Cajuns seared everything in cast iron it seemed.

'Alexander, my man, saw you on TV in DC with that trade deal. Good to see you alive and back home for a change.'

Senator Thibodaux smiled and leaned back, 'looking forward to a relaxing weekend and some big fish Michael.'

Adam was scurrying about and fetched Michael another cold beer, he handed one to Ted who obediently put down his water bottle and smiled his thanks. Adam was gone in a second with the empty bottle.

Brad had jumped up and climbed to the bridge. 'Alex you want to take off now or are we waiting on anything?'

Alex turned in his chair towards the bridge, 'You're the Captain, Brad, you want to get out ahead go for it. We are happy to enjoy a few drinks and enjoy the ride.'

Brad said, 'let's get on down river to Port Edes, it's a 27-mile run, and Lucky is saving me a slip. Shotgun start at midnight, but we can run out in the gulf and catch some dinner come back to the dock.

Alex turned back to Ted and Michael and said, 'Get comfortable, I think we are about to take off. Brad is very competitive; he was not joking about that at all.'

Ted felt the deck beneath him vibrate as the Cummins diesel engines roared to life and Brad shouted instructions at Adam to untie the boat. He expertly pulled the boat out of the slip and in seconds was out in the channel leading away from the marina. Michael smashed his empty beer can and got another for himself while Adam was busy and sat back down.

'Alex, what are we looking at with NAFTA signed now?' asked Michael.

'Unlimited trading in effect immediately. We need a good look at the seafood market to see where our interests are best served. I'm hoping Ted here, will go back to Texas and come back to see us with an investment from his Grandfather that will result in immediate profits with our friends from Mexico.'

'That is great news. I know how profitable the redfish ban has been for your Mississippi friends and I'm looking forward to cashing in on the snapper. I wish my buddy from Tampa had been able to join us this weekend. I wanted him to talk to you about the market further east in the gulf. Redfish are it and a bag of chips here in Louisiana and Texas right now thanks to the bag limits but further over the larger market share is snapper and stone crabs. In all the fish houses and tourist dives over that way the Yankee's don't give a shit what it costs, they just want sunshine and seafood.'

'Well anyone who wants to part with their money is certainly able to exercise that right in America!' Alex retorted with a laugh. 'All we need to do is bring the needed fish in through Mexico. We do not make any money off our local commercial fisherman.'

The yacht powered through the channels and headed down the Mississippi on the way to the gulf.

'What is the difference between redfish and red snapper?' Ted asked looking at Michael.

'Snapper is a lean firm white meat, that lends itself well to cooking of all kinds, it's good baked in multiple ethnic casserole style dishes, it's especially good pan seared and even grilled because the meat is firm and holds up to cooking that way. It complements what it is cooked and served with. Redfish is a common name and they are a deep-sea rockfish in the same species. We can ask Brad. The issue is really the size and the bag limits. Based on supply and demand.

When Bush signed the redfish ban the prices went through the roof thanks to my good buddy from Opelousas who had all of America wanting to eat fish burned in spices and butter! Good stuff!'

Michael laughed all the way to the cooler and grabbed another cold one as the yacht sped further down the river.

'Do y'all want to fish tonight? Maybe catch dinner? We have steaks if you don't want to fish tonight.' Brad hollered down from the bridge.

'Oh, we can make a down or two and see what happens.' Michael hollered back, 'tell Adam to have the grill ready and I'll grill whatever we catch or the steaks if we don't catch a damn fish!'

'We can ease up on a rig and make a few downs. If we catch a decent fish or two, we can cook dinner on board.' Brad had piloted into the mouth of the gulf and headed towards a near shore oil rig. He got the Reel Good in position based on the wind and current and told Adam to drop anchor.

Brad checked Adam's anchor and was satisfied with his deck hands work so he directed him to fetch the fishing rods and pre-baited gear. Adam returned to the deck with four six oughts' on stand-up rods. Ted felt his excitement rise. He grabbed a pole and stood beside Brad on the starboard side of the Reel Good. They were facing towards the oil rig and Ted could see some rig workers watching them through binoculars. 'don't mind them, they fish all the time from these rigs after shift. Most of these guys probably rather be out here than home. But we are a welcome sight and amusing for them to watch.'

Ted nodded and decided the best way for him not to look like an idiot would be to follow Brad's instructions. Brad told him to drop his line and slowly count to thirty and lock it off. Ted felt a tug and told Brad he had a bite. 'don't yank!' Brad said, 'Let him swallow the bait and hook good before you yank it out of his mouth... easy...easy...feel the play?'

Ted nodded again; he wanted this fish so bad he could already taste him! Brad reached over and gave a gentle pull on Ted's line. 'Okay! Your set! Yank him in!'

Ted cranked the reel and leaned back. He must have hooked a whale was his first thought as the line went tight and he had to lean and crank with all his strength. The battle between fish and man was on and by the time Ted got the thrashing fish close enough for Brad to gaff him his arms were on fire from the fight.

Brad hauled the fish over the rails and shouted, 'Dinner is on board boys! Whooooweee!'

Ted's first catch was a 21-pound snapper. 'Oh man!' hollered Michael, 'that one is going to live on as a legend in my frying pan!' Brad was holding up the fish with one arm and smacked Ted on the shoulder. Ted winced. His arms and shoulders were not feeling as good as his attitude and appetite even as he basked in the admiration of his fish.

Michael and Alex were getting beat on the port side but then the reels started screaming for help. Alex grabbed a pole and began his own war between man and fish. The war was waged and finally Adam was able to gaff the senator's fish, a forty plus pound amberjack.

'Hot DAMN, it's gonna be good eats tonight!' yelled Michael, grabbing another beer. 'shots for the fisherman!' he continued, pouring up a finger of scotch for Alex and Ted. Alex turned towards Ted and touched his shot glass to his and said, 'Cheers mate! Good work!' Ted was warm with euphoria and the scotch as he smiled at the senator and gulped the scotch.

Everyone admired the two fish and Brad told Adam to go ahead and fillet them out while he piloted the yacht back to the dock at Port Edes. Adam, silent and fast, scurried off again to fetch fillet knives and cutting board.

Ted wanted to fish more; he had the fever now. But he was a guest and would comply with whatever Alex said. Alex was in charge of this show.

Alex said, 'why don't we have some dinner and see what happens? We head out after the bills, in the morning, right?'

Brad chimed in, 'Yes so anymore reds or jacks will have to go in the box. These fish won't count towards our bag limit. I would like for you and Ted to have some nice ones to freeze and take home, we could limit out right here in this spot tonight, but we have big money riding on this tournament tomorrow.'

Ted sat down, he was shaking with excitement from his catch and the scotch, it just dawned on him how very hungry he was. 'We can eat some fresh fish, that sounds Reel Good to me!' He joked. Everyone joined in and Michael and Adam started clapping and chanting, 'Reel Good! Reel Good!' as everyone laughed. Michael produced a fresh round of shot glasses full of scotch, 'to the Reel Good!' He toasted.

Brad backed into the slip at Port Edes and Adam tied her off. Brad hustled down the deck and pulled the cover off of what turned out to be a professional grill mounted on the back deck.

Adam reappeared and handed Michael a tray of perfectly cut fish fillets. Alex said, 'Let's blacken that snapper and grill the amberjack, can you handle that Michael?' Michael grabbed the tray and grinned. 'you got it! Time for me to get to work boys!' He told Adam to get the table ready and gracefully bounded down the stairs to the galley to season the fillets.

Ted sat beside Alex and watched all this activity with a deep pleasure. It was calm and peaceful at the dock now. The sounds of activity from the oil rig seemed to be coming from miles away and were a pleasant backdrop to the sound of waves slapping on the bottom of the boat. There was a light breeze blowing and the unbearable humidity of New Orleans was a distant memory.

Adam reappeared, silently as always, with a tray containing a roll of paper towels, knives, forks, salt, pepper and hot sauce. Michael Brandon's brand of course.

He turned to the elder senator and asked if he could fix him another cocktail. Alex smiled, 'of course, thank you.'


'I can't wait!' said Ted, excited as a little boy on Christmas Eve. 'are the bills as easy as the snapper and amberjack? This just seemed too easy this evening?' He had conveniently forgotten his aching arms with the glow of the scotch in his system.

'No, right here it's the rigs. The oil rigs make the perfect artificial reefs, and this is where the fish like to congregate. The bills do come in here occasionally to eat but they are mainly open water fish, much further offshore. I tell you what' continued Brad, 'Next time you are in the City of New Orleans and have a few hours to kill go to the Aquarium of the America's. They have a gulf exhibit that recreates the underwater atmosphere we just fished between these rigs. It's huge and shows the food chain perfectly. The tiny fish school around the pilings, feasting on barnacles and algae chased by the bigger fish, who are also chased by bigger fish like the ones we just caught and the sharks circle to catch them. The food chain in action, without us messing it up!'

Michael appeared from below decks with the tray of now perfectly seasoned fillets followed by Adam carrying two huge cast iron skillets. 'Is the fire ready?'

Brad got up and checked the grill. 'Yeah, put the pans on and when you're ready slap 'em on there. I'm hungry!'

Adam set the skillets on the grill and then placed two plastic containers on the table. One contained a fresh salad and the other was smoked tuna dip. Ted's mouth started watering and Adam stuck a spoon in the dip and a box of crackers magically appeared on the table. Adam opened the crackers and spread them out on a paper plate. 'You try?' he bowed and waved the cracker plate at Ted. 'This good appetizer.'

Ted gratefully grabbed a cracker and spread the enticing dip on it and popped it into his mouth. His taste buds light up with the smoky fishy taste on the buttery cracker and he knew he could make a meal out of this dip alone.

'That there is another example of gold in a bucket.' Said Michael, grabbing a cracker and sticking it in the dip. 'The fisherman won't sell us their tuna that don't grade high because we can grab them for a few dollars a pound. When we do get a Captain, whose had a bad trip and has only low grades we buy it, smoke it and chop it up for dips and sell the dips for as much as the high-grade tuna. It's a glorious racket! And don't it taste good!' He laughed.

Ted could not stop eating the wonderful smoked tuna dip. This would sell in Texas like barrels of oil.

'Brad you said the rigs were the key? The underwater environment attracts the fish and makes them hang around here?'

'yeah that is pretty much it. Off the coast of Louisiana there is offshore drilling so lots of rigs make up an artificial reef system. It's a little different further east. That white sand your wife loves in Destin. It's what is on the bottom of the gulf too. It's a damn dessert of white sand all the way out. The fish have no place to congregate so they keep swimming till they find a place. The Destin boys are successful because they know this and have built artificial reefs all over the gulf that are covered with fish. You can fish and catch good game fish here just by going out till you see a rig and make a down. In Alabama and Florida, the fisherman build their own reefs and keep the locations secret. If you don't have reef locations in your GPS, you ain't catching a fish.'

Ted thought about this and said, 'So if it's the reefs that make the fishing possible how do the fisherman make a reef?'

Brad looked thoughtfully at the young state representative. 'Well, they are made from old cars, washing machines and scrap metal type stuff. But it's not littering or hauling trash out to dump. The items are carefully chosen, cleansed of pollutants and placed out in the gulf where the barnacles and small crustaceans attach to form a reef. We have a guy in Destin who is the best at it. Most of the Captains pay him to make reefs. I can't scratch up my yacht hauling a wrecked car out there and I don't want to. My job is to take people out, show them a good time on a nice boat and catch fish. Captain Farrell has a reputation in Destin and his deckhands say he has read every code, book and regulation so he's schooled in how to do this. The reefs produce tons of fish, but the coast guard is on his ass all the time.'

Michael lifted the hood off the grill and a cloud of steam went up in a sizzle as he smacked the fillets on the hot iron. Ted was full of tuna dip, but the aroma of sizzling fish, butter, garlic and other spices made his mouth start watering all over again. He filed away the name of the reef building Captain he had just heard in his mental rolodex. He had a feeling he would need to know it soon.

Michael plopped down thick paper plates with the cooked fish fillets. The aromatic spices drifted up and teased the noses and taste buds of the hungry men. Ted looked at the plates. Thick fillets hung over the sides of the paper plates and were glistening hot and steaming. On one side of the fish that hogged the plate was a creamy sauce Michael had whipped up with little chunks of crab meat and diced tomato and scallions. It was the perfect companion to the spicy fish and Ted grabbed his knife and fork as Michael yelled, 'Bon appetite my fish killing brethren!' Michael sank into the chair between Brad and Alex and grabbed his own knife and fork.

Alex dug in with obvious appreciation as Michael folded a huge chunk of blackened snapper into his mouth and chewed. He sighed in enjoyment. He then turned to Ted and said, 'grouper is also excellent blackened and smoked. I love fish. I do not know why I am so fat...'

Ted was too busy forking the delicious fish into his own mouth to point out the obvious as Michael hollered for Adam to bring him another beer. Adam fixed drinks and waters for the men at the table then sank cross legged on the deck with a huge plate of his own.

The men ate in appreciative silence for a few minutes then Brad spoke up. 'So early AM we'll take off deeper and dredge for bills. If we get lucky, we can head on in and weigh in the winner. If not, we'll stay all night in the gulf. We have till about 4pm Sunday to bring one in and get to the scales.'

Sounds good Brad, we leave that up to your capable hands.' Replied Alex as he wiped his mouth.

'Get some rest tonight boys, tomorrow it's war! I'm hitting my bunk.' Said the Captain as he existed into the salon.

Daybreak on the Gulf of Mexico is a special kind of beautiful. Most people would say, 'what is there to see? It's only water everywhere?' In the absence of civilization, the awareness of God is enhanced by the sunrise splashing the water with colors unseen by most human eyes. A wisp or two of clouds add to the beauty as they change colors from dark grey to golden red, to gold to yellow then finally to white fluff over deep blue water. The peace that permeates a soul as the sun rises in the east to paint the skies over the vast waters can only be captured by experiencing it in person.

Michael Brandon stumbled out onto the back deck with a piece of cold amberjack in his hand. Adam had two pots of black coffee ready to go, along with alka seltzer and water bottles.

Then Adam broke out the big game tackle, 7 rods of war with outriggers laid out and the spread set in order. Captain Brad yelled down from the bridge, 'Game on boys! Hook 'em high!'


Alex came up and stood beside Ted on the port side as they watched the teasers bounce on top of the water. 'So, son, I am hoping that even though your grandfather does not appreciate fish to the extent you do you can convince him that now is the time to invest in it. I know the man does like money!'

Yes sir, that is a family trait, I can assure you! Tell me what you want from him and I will get it.' Ted refused to break his gaze into the Senators eyes. His intensity was undeniable.


'We need to sponsor our own fishing fleet, run out of Mexico to sell the fish to our American markets. Mexican Captains will work off the price of a boat no matter how long it takes, their deckhands work for pennies compared to American's and with the no trade tariffs and no bag limits in their waters, Michael and our other importers will make huge profits we will all share in.'

Ted smiled as the senator continued, 'What I need is someone who is not connected to the NAFTA agreement to fund the fleet to get it going and I'm sure with the profits made your grandfather will make a generous donation to my re-election campaign.'

Ted's smile turned into a grin, 'Sir, I can promise you my grandfather's cooperation. And I will fund the first boat myself.'

Alex raised his eyebrows at the younger man. 'Oh, I have a little fund hidden away from my wife that I've been waiting to put into an investment project of my own. I just found it.' Ted informed the older man.

Both men started laughing as they shook hands in the salt spray.

# Chapter 5

*FORT WALTON BEACH, FLORIDA*

The phone rang in the Department of Natural Resources Office.

Regina Bates heard it ring but ignored it. She was composing an email to her one and only friend, Dr. Peter B. Garcia PHD at West Florida University. Regina had been trying to secure him further grant money and had found another grant of $86,000 in funding to determine if fish are actually attracted to artificial reefs or do they simply reproduce and populate the reefs?

Ms. Bates? Call for you please?'

Regina was a very small, unimposing woman but her staff at the DNR feared her temper and vindictiveness. When angered her short stringy hair seemed to fluff out in a greyish cloud and her tiny brown eyes became huge and magnified behind her wire rim glasses that perched on a horrifically beaked nose over pale lips that never saw a hint of lipstick. She would puff up and appear much larger than her five-foot frame and gave off the appearance of an angry wet hen. She was well known to make people's jobs disappear out of revenge.

It seemed that Ms. Bates hated fisherman despite her own master's degree in marine biology and her work with the government on behalf of fisherman. This was a huge mystery as her own father had been a boat builder and fisherman, as had his father and his father and so on. Ms. Bates had spent her entire life in Florida on the water.

Ms. Bates looked up and peered at the sycophant who disturbed her sanctuary office.

'Who is it? And what do they want?' she snapped at the terrified young man.

'It's a Senator from Texas Ma'am.'

'Oh well tell him I will be on the phone in approximately 3 minutes.'

She went back to her computer screen. She would share her good news regarding the grant she had secured for Peter's continued research on fish mating before she spoke with anyone.

Finally, she picked up the phone and said with artificial sweetness, 'This is Ms. Bates, how may I assist you today?'

'Mrs. Bates, this is Senator Theodore Hollis calling you from Texas, how are you today ma'am?'

'It is MS. Bates and I am fine Senator, what is it I can do for you?'

'Certainly Ms. Bates' Ted tried not to laugh, Alex had warned him this female was a ball buster and very power hungry. 'I wanted to speak to you today over some concerns Senator Alex Thibodaux and I have over the building of artificial reefs in the Gulf of Mexico and how that relates to the fishing population. As you know Texas and Louisiana are very concerned about protecting our Gulf from overfishing by commercial fisherman and protecting our native fish stock and the Gulf environment.'

Regina Bates sat up straight. Her brown eyes had become very large behind her thick glasses.

'Yes, Senator, protecting our Gulf is my top concern. What exactly is it you need done?'

Ted spoke with Regina for seven more minutes and when Regina hung up the phone her brown eyes were huge, and her thin lips stretched in something that resembled a smile on a chicken.

In Texas, Ted smiled. Alex had as usual, been right on the money about who to use. Ted knew he had the right fish on his line to further their agenda. Ms. Bates would prove to be very useful indeed.

There were two men Regina Bates absolutely despised, the first was her own father. The second was a Captain in Destin who not only ran charters but built artificial reefs and had made her out to be a total fool.

Regina's first run in with Captain Matthew Farrell had been at a city-wide meeting she called in Destin over artificial reef building. She had gotten members of the EPA, Corp of Engineers, Coast Guard and her buddy Pete to form a panel and had local Captains sign in on a log where the Captains had to sign in with name, years of experience and name of their vessel as well as how many artificial reefs they had either built or had access to. Ms. Bates had then attached this 'log' to a letter to the Federal Government stating the local Captains did not want to build artificial reefs but wanted the government to take over. When Ms. Bates announced at the follow up meeting that she was using the Captains data to encourage the Federal Government to take over any reef building Captain Farrell had jumped up and yelled, 'you called this meeting under false pretenses! You had us sign in and used it as our death warrants taking this information back to Tallahassee to further your own personal agenda. If we can't build reefs we can't fish and that puts us out of business. This may just be politics to you lady, but to us working men we call it what it is, LIES and BULL.'

The ensuing ruckus from the coastal community Captains after this ensured that Ms. Bates was watched and questioned by these Captains and could not get any of them to sign another document or back her pet projects.

Regina's second run in with Captain Farrell had been when she tried to impose fines on him using the Marpol Act for putting plastic in the gulf. It was painfully obvious that she was trying to get revenge after the reef meeting fiasco. She had called Captain Farrell to her office with the intention of humiliating him in front of her staff.

However, Captain Farrell had informed her he would never use plastic but suggested that Ms. Bates and her beloved project with the WFU of placing plastic fertilizer cones in the Choctawhatchee Bay may be a violation she might want to investigate. He then informed her that she had wasted 86,000 dollars studying fish mating as fish cannot possibly mate on a reef unless they are attracted to it.

Regina's cheeks burned red hot as she recalled her then secretary giggling at this horrid Captain who had the nerve to go on and tell her that for the 86,000 dollars she had wasted he could have built her an artificial reef of her very own in the Gulf the size of the state capital Building in Tallahassee.

Regina eyed the aquarium in her office and wished she had been able to force feed one of her poisonous lionfish to that damn Captain before he walked out of her office. She fired the secretary immediately.

Regina pushed away from the desk and got up. Her office was so cluttered with shelving laden down with books, small creatures that had experienced taxidermy and aquariums there was only one path from her desk to the door. She was small woman, so it was plenty of room for her to pace. So, pace she did.

Her next encounter with Captain Farrell was over white goods. White goods were washers, dryers, refrigerators, etc.... that the local fisherman were using to make small fishing reefs with. Regina had been on a personal mission to outlaw this pollution of the gulf and had personally called Captain Farrell to inform him that she was closely monitoring reef material.

Captain Farrell had asked her what her problem was with an old washer being used as a reef base? She instructed him that washers could tumble across the gulf floor tearing up thousands of years' worth of sedimentation and destroying the food chain at its most elementary level. There was a pause and this damned Captain has asked her if she was sitting down?

'For what?' she snapped, 'I'm personally telling you to stop putting garbage out in the gulf!'

'Ms. Bates, do you have any idea how a shrimp net operates? They have two 1000-pound doors on either side of a 50ft. chain that they drag on the ocean floor plowing up the gulf bottom for 25 miles at a stretch to catch shrimp. I don't think my cleaned out, door less washers that may tip over when I place them on the ocean floor are destroying the food chain at its most elementary level. Call me when you have an enforceable law on the books.' He then hung up on her.

Regina's cheeks flushed flaming hot again at this memory. She knew exactly who Senator Alex Thibodaux was and she did a quick online search on Ted Hollis. He may only be a state senator, but he had a powerful family and even more powerful friends. With politicians like these on her side, making life miserable for the gulf captains would be a cake walk.

She pictured Captain Farrell's smug face in her office and thought, 'I'm going to shut him down for good!'

The implications of what Senator Hollis implied that they were interested in protecting the sports fisherman over commercials also excited her greatly. 'I have a real problem with fisherman who build reefs for the sole purpose of catching a fish.' She muttered out loud as she dialed a number.

She got one of Peter's grad students to tell Dr. Garcia she was on her way to take him for a celebration lunch.

Regina sat on the board of the Marine Fisheries Council, she, along with four other board members controlled a fifth of American food sales with bag limits on fish. They were a powerful board, indeed and Pete would be able to use his data to help her convince the other board members of the MFC to call for even tighter bag limits in the gulf.

As she left for her celebratory lunch with her only friend, Regina Bates informed her secretary to set up a meeting for her with the Destin Harbor Master.

'I want him here in my office tomorrow morning, no excuses!' she snapped as she stormed out of the office trying not to smile. Smiling would ruin her reputation.

# Chapter 6



Regina Bates head was swimming. She downed two Goody powders with Mountain Dew, an old fisherman's remedy for the splitting headache that comes along with a colossal hangover. Regina was not a big drinker but yesterday she and Pete had downed several Rum Runners with smoked tuna dip prior to ordering actual food. There were multiple little paper umbrellas on the table before the Captain's Platters arrived loaded down with fried gulf shrimp, slabs of fried grouper, oysters, calamari and seasoned fries. For some reason huge quantities of fried food makes you feel like your sobering up a bit, so you order more drinks. Her lunch with Pete ended over key lime cheesecake and champagne at sunset.

Pete was ecstatic that his little bird like friend had secured him further grant funding for his grouper mating project. Another $86K meant he would not have to worry about having to teach the students at WFU anytime soon. Those damn kids asking questions he could not answer irritated him to no end.

Regina was ecstatic that Pete would use his research to help her call for tighter bag limits and screw the gulf's fishing Captains. She could just picture several of the Destin Captains hung in a big fish net gasping for air and begging her for mercy. This fantasy made her hangover well worth it and she relished the mental image of the men in a fish net.

Now for the Harbor Master.

The Destin Harbor Master was a nice title, but no real authority to go with it. However, Regina knew just how to manipulate this situation. Bo Calhoun was from an old line of Destin's founding fisherman, but he could not fish. He got horribly seasick just watching the tide come in and the smell of fish however fresh, made him gag.

He was the black sheep of his family because of these deficiency's and had been given the Harbor Master job so he could stay on land and not embarrass the family.

He shuffled into Regina Bates office and took his hat off. He didn't dare sit down till she looked up and waved her hand at him. He had had runs in with Ms. Bates before.

'Bo, how are you today?' she finally looked up and said, 'sit down.'

She took a huge gulp of her Mountain Dew and started giving Bo his instructions.

Bo left relieved, all she wanted him to do was stay on the harbor and watch out for the Reef Runner. Just call the Coast Guard every time Captain Farrell took off with a load of reef building material and let her know. That should be easy enough.

And Regina had promised him that his 'policing the waters to prevent pollution' would get his picture on the front page of the Destin Log. That would help get his mother and brothers off his back about being a failure in the family business.

He smiled and headed back to the Harbor. Maybe Ms. Bates wasn't so bad after all he thought.

## *CORTEZ, FLORIDA*

Ted sipped on an ice-cold corona at the Tide Tables restaurant enjoying the ocean breeze on his back. His wife, Mellie was standing in line to go to the lady's room with a huge smile on her face. She had a new pair of Chanel sunglasses gracing her beautiful face and a drink with an umbrella stuck in an orange wedge in her hand. She was chatting with another tourist in line about how charming the historic fishing village was and that her husband was taking her shopping in Sarasota after they ate.

Ted watched his wife with a smile on his face.

He was feeling very generous today after watching his fishing boat unload a very profitable load of grouper, tile fish, red snapper and scamp at Teller Fish Company. Mellie had no idea why her husband was so interested in watching the Captain oversee the fish house rep monitor the weights as the deckhands yelled in Spanish and threw fish after fish on the conveyor belt that moved the fish to the scales. But she stood there smiling in her new designer glasses, indulging Ted.

Ted had not spoken to Mellie much today; his mind was too preoccupied with his secret boat and the success of this venture so far.

Mellie disappeared into the lady's room and the tank top clad waitress plopped a paper boat of crab cakes and come back sauce in front of Ted with a round platter of ice and a dozen fresh shucked oysters.

'Nother beer?' her smile was direct and open with Mellie away from the table. Ted smiled back and said, 'hell yes, and one of those fruity things for my wife.' He winked and the waitress laughed and took off to the bar. Ted could not resist an appreciative quick glance at her well stuffed cut off shorts. 'Grandpa would be slapping that!' he chuckled.

Ted flashed back to walking Mellie away from the Fish House this morning after the Captain gave him the thumbs up. 'So, if the boat makes 2.75 to 3.00 a pound and the boat grossed 13 thousand pounds, that equals \$39K minus expenses of the boat leaving about \$35K profit. Damn!' He slapped one hand on the table scooping up a crab cake and dipping it in the delicious come back sauce with the other hand.

Ted popped the fried, dripping cake in his mouth and almost moaned out loud with pleasure as the concoction of cornmeal, eggs and huge chucks of sweet crab meat dissolved on his tongue.

Watching Mellie head back to their table he flashed back to the fishing trip with Senator Thibodeau and heard Michael Brandon laughing in his head, 'But the real killing is when 4 ounces of that fish goes for $20 plate at a restaurant my boy! Then your fish is actually going for $80 a pound.'

Mellie sat down and squealed and opened her perfectly glossed lips for Ted to pop a chuck of dripping crab cake in her mouth.

'Ted! That is fabulous! We don't eat like this in Texas honey. I'm sure this is not on my diet. I came with you to get tanned not fat!'

Ted smiled, 'Baby I don't think you have a fat gene in your body. You can just play some extra sets of tennis when we get home. I have an idea to run by you.'

The waitress plopped the fresh drinks down and Mellie squealed again, 'Teddy, what are you up to trying to get me drunk?'

'Well you and the ladies do such great work with shelters and stuff like that, what if you had a restaurant like this that gave your shelter people jobs? You could just manage it, can you see it, Mellie's Florida Fish House, employing the needy and getting them back into society. The press will LOVE you for it! You won't have to pay for any advertising'

Mellie's hand was frozen on her way to her mouth holding an oyster.

'Ted! I love it! But a restaurant? Can we afford it? That is one big investment to do it right?'

The waitress returned and plopped down the 'catch of the day' platter.

Ted glanced down at the steaming hot fillets of fish fresh out of the deep fryer and smiled at his wife. He folded up the paper menu and handed it to Mellie, 'Here stuff this in your purse, money won't be a problem. Just enjoy this and we will go walk it off at the mall and talk about your new venture.'

The afternoon was waning fast, but Captain Matt was feeling good. Charles had all the cars on the deck prepped, ready and tied down and they were sinking 6 reef's tonight. Good payday this week, he smiled. He decided he would surprise Donna and the kids with a trip to Zoo World in Panama City this weekend. That would make Donna happy as there would be plenty of places for her to take cute pictures of the kids. Matt knew he had never taken the kids there; he wasn't sure if Donna had chaperoned a field trip there or not, but this had all the makings of a perfect family day. Donna would be very happy with him. He smiled.

'Capt., you ready?'

Matt gave Charles the nod and Charles threw off the bow line and Matt pulled the Reef Runner out of the slip. He spotted Bo Calhoun standing on the next dock, doing his best to look very official with his binoculars and radio strapped to his belt.

Matt also spotted a reporter for the Destin Log taking pictures of the Harbor. She seemed to be focusing on tourists struggling to bring a jet ski in.

'Bo!' he shouted, 'turn around' Matt pantomimed taking a picture as Bo stared, confused. Then Matt picked up his own binoculars and yelled, 'turn around Bo!'

Bo finally got it and raised his binoculars in one hand and snatched his radio off his belt. He did a one-legged Captain Morgan pose on a piling and "snap" the reporter got a picture of the Destin Harbor Master, looking very official for the front page.

Matt laughed and headed out the pass to his profitable evening. He said a prayer of thanks and thought about how cute Abby was going to look squealing with delight as she saw her first real bear up close.

The phone rang in Regina Bates office, but she ignored it. She had run a paperclip through the gills of a feeder guppy and was teasing her lionfish with it. Her eyes were large as she imagined Captain Farrell was the guppy and she was the lionfish closing in for the kill.

'Ms. Bates?'

Regina dropped the string tied to her paperclip fishhook. 'What?' she snapped as she whirled away from the aquarium and fixed the frightened young man with her huge eyes.

'Call for you from the Harbor Master ma'am. It's five o'clock ma'am. I'll see you tomorrow'

Regina ignored the young man. For some reason she liked him, it must have been the aftershave of fear he left in his wake and he fled out the door.

She snatched the phone up, 'Yes?' she snapped.

'Ms. Bates, it's Bo. Calhoun. Ma'am.'

'I know your name Bo, what it is it?'

'I just wanted to let you know the Reef Runner just left her slip headed out the pass and I called the Coast Guard like you asked.'

'What was on board?' She asked.

'Crushed cars ma'am. Looks like he is doing some reefs this evening.'

'Good work Bo. What did the Coast Guard say when you called them?'

'They are going to follow him and check it out ma'am.'

'Thank you, Bo, good work!' She hung up on Bo and started laughing. Regina decided to run a paperclip through another feeder guppy, but she was laughing so hard she could not catch one.

# Chapter 7



*DESTIN, FLORIDA*

Captain Matt was in his shop on Mountain Drive in Destin. He was fabricating a fuel tank for a 50-foot commercial fishing boat out of fiberglass material to lighten the ships weight. His shop neighbor Don was watching and armchair quarterbacking the fabrication process.

Matt had no intention of glassing the fabricated tank till Don got bored and left, once he started, he had to finish the entire thing to make sure the glass was smooth and even. As Don yammered on about something, Matt nodded and thought he should have brought Charles in to help with this. Charles loved to sniff fiberglass resin and he would roll it smooth as silk till all the smell was gone with a smile on his face.

Just then Matt's pager went off on his desk. Matt walked over and saw it had a '10' on the tiny screen.

Donna and Matt had codes set up and 8 was call when you have a chance, 9 was call as soon as possible and 10 meant 911- call NOW.

Matt waved his arm at Don and said, 'I got to call the wife.'

Donna answered the house phone before it rang and started screaming and crying, Matt's heart was doing a tap dance in his chest. 'Matt the FBI was here looking for you!' she managed to get out.

'Crap Donna! I thought one of the kids had been run over!'

'But Matt, the FBI! What is going on? What do they want? Why did they come here?'

'Donna! Calm down! First of all, how do you even know it was the FBI?'

Donna continued to gasp and tried to catch her breath. Matt was trying but he was losing his patience with her quickly. Now that he knew the kids and Donna were not headed to an emergency room somewhere, he just wanted to know what was going on and get back to this fuel tank.

'Donna, did they drive an FBI car? Or were they wearing FBI clothes? How do you KNOW it was the FBI and not some idiot trying to sell magazines?'

Donna got angry at this point and snapped, 'They showed me a badge and gave me a business card. YOU call this guy!'

She spat the number out at Matt and hung up the phone.

Matt looked at the phone in disbelief, she was more upset than he had realized. His brownie points from the surprise zoo trip were out the window now.

He sighed and dialed the number he had scribbled down while on the phone with Donna.

'Special Agent Mitchell Ruby here'

'Um yes, this is Matt Farrell, I just got a message from my wife that you came by and wanted to speak with me?'

'I am interested in your artificial reef building.' Responded Agent Ruby dryly.

'Oh sure, do you want a reef built?' Matt took a deep breath, this was nothing. He had built reefs for several lawyers, judges and a couple of senators, this guy probably just liked to fish too.

'I'm at my shop over on Mountain Dr. If you were just at my house, it's only about 10 minutes away.' Matt gave him the address and hung up. He was visibly relieved. Don was still standing there taking it all in. The man loved good gossip more than a hairdresser.

Matt walked back over to his sawhorses and looked at the fuel tank. Today had been full of interruptions and he was about to point out to Don the sign by the door that said: 'your first 10 minutes are free, after that $20 per 15-minute increments for my time!'

Matt knew he could not activate the resin till Don left and he estimated about 3 hours to glass this tank.

Just then a black Crown Victoria pulled up and squealed to a stop in front of the open bay door of Matt's shop.

As Matt and Don stood there watching the driver's door opened very slowly and a tall, lanky man with thinning blonde hair wearing dark Ray Ban's got out. Matt's first thought was, 'he's wearing a black suit and a tie in Destin? He is going to melt that tie off.'

The man just stood there staring at Matt for a long moment.

Then he slowly reached into the car, got a briefcase out and walked up to the two men. 'I am Special Agent Mitchell Ruby and I am here to speak with Mr. Matthew Farrell about artificial reef building activity.'

Don started stammering, 'Matt, I have to go buddy.'

Matt said, 'Well Don I guess you do, and I guess I'm here talking to the FBI!'

Don ran off looking back over his shoulder. Matt sighed; he knew Don would be on the phone telling God only knew who about this before he could make another pot of coffee.

Matt turned to Agent Ruby and said, 'well would you like to step in here? You can use my desk, your welcome to it.'

Agent Ruby walked over to Matt's desk and placed his briefcase on it, then he slowly walked around to the chair and sat down. Matt noticed that Agent Ruby seemed to be like a portrait in a Mexican restaurant. His eyes never left Matt's. Finally, the tall agent sat down, opened the briefcase and pulled out a leather notepad flips through it and says, 'Okay tell me about July 3, 1993.'

Matt thought 'wahhhhaaat?' Now Matt felt the first tingling of uncertainty start crawling around in his belly. 'Um okay, what about it?'

Agent Ruby repeated, 'tell me about July 3, 1993.'

Matt said cheerfully, 'Well it's one day before July 4th!'

Agent Ruby scowled and said, 'One Mr. John Barber, a special investigator with the Coast Guard pursued a case against you for $250,000 in fines over reef building material.'

Matt said, 'Well that suit was dismissed without prejudice. That is over with, it's long been resolved I did nothing wrong building those reefs.'

Agent Ruby, 'No it's not, that was civil I am federal and I'm looking into it.'

Matt sighed, 'Look man, let me come around there and open some drawers in my desk. I have paper copies of everything you need to clear up whatever this is in my files. And behind you are some of my permits framed. But I've got copies of everything in my locked file drawer beside where you are sitting, ok?'

Agent Ruby pushed back in the roller chair and waved his arms like a conductor over the desk. 'By all means, show me what you have.'

Matt carefully stepped around the desk beside the simmering FBI agent and opened his file drawer. He pulled out the documentation giving him the permit to build reefs from the Army Corp of Engineers where the permit builder had permission to contract this work out with a letter of authority from the permit holder.

Agent Ruby snatched the papers from Matt and snapped, 'your name is not on this permit.'

Matt tried to explain to the agent that his name was on the notarized permission document to use this permit and showed him the letter issued by the SAJ-50.

Agent Ruby continued, 'this is NOT your permit!' He was getting red in the face and angry.

Matt explained again, 'Look my name is on the notarized permission document that references this permit with the permit license number. I am legally able to use this permit as laid out in the guidelines from the Corp of Engineers!'

Agent Ruby continued to state, 'Your name is not on this permit!' as he scribbled frantically on the legal pad glaring at Matt the entire time.

Matt took a deep breath and tried again to explain to the agent that he had personally worked on the SAJ-50 committee to establish guidelines for safe and friendly environmental reef building and his notarized letter gave him permission to use the permit.

Agent Ruby refused to acknowledge anything Matt was saying as he scribbled frantically on his notepad.

Matt was getting little nervous and he thought, 'This will stand up in a court of law. I helped design these rules with the board for the safety of all involved with artificial reef building board, I don't know why this FBI man seems to have it in for me, but I'm ok. I have obeyed the law to the letter.'

Matt took a deep breath and said, 'Mr. Ruby, can this stuff your writing down be used against me in a court of law?

Agent Ruby puffed up and stated, 'of course it can! This is an investigation! And you are to address me as Agent Ruby...' He glared at Matt.

Matt felt a strange peace spreading inside his chest and folded his arms and said calmly, 'Well that is it then, I have nothing further to say. I'm not sticking my head in any noose; I'm not sucking on a loaded gun. You do what you have to do to investigate me. I know I am operating within the laws, so you do what you have to do. I just ask you to not make this personal. You've got a job to do, but if you make it personal it's not a job anymore.'

Agent Ruby's frustration and mounting fury was obvious as he stood up and slammed his legal pad down.

Matt continued 'look man, my conscious is clear on artificial reef building. I did everything I could do to ensure it was done safely and providing work and benefits to our economy to make it productive. I don't feel guilty about anything I have done and my conscious is not bothering me at all.'

Agent Ruby was very red in the face now and states, 'We can do this the hard way, or we can do this the easy way!'

Matt said, 'what is the guaranteed outcome on the easy way?'

Agent Ruby snarled, 'There is not one.'

Matt shrugged and marveled at the peace he felt and said, 'Well let's let the chips fall where they may then. Look at my hands, I work for a living. You get out there and do what you have to do. I'm not going to help you!'

Agent Ruby saw clearly that Captain Matt was not going to crucify himself for him he got very upset and grabbed his yellow pad up and stomped to the front of the shop and as he got to the door he turned around, pointed his finger at Matt and said, 'Let me tell you something. I don't give up; I don't quit, and you better believe I'll be back.'

And he stormed through the doors Matt cheerfully said, 'Well I hope so. You left your briefcase under my desk!'

Agent Ruby made his walk of shame back to the desk as Matt tried to stifle his laughter at the man's obvious discomfort.

Matt knew he was now at the top of this man's S- list, the bullseye on his dart board... but it was, what it was...

Matt said a brief prayer thanking God for the supernatural peace that had permeated his being. It had to be supernatural. How else does one stay so calm with an armed furious FBI agent sitting at your desk with his car blocking your exit at your shop. And thinking of Agent Ruby getting so frustrated and angry he walked off without his briefcase set Matt off laughing.

Still laughing he decided to call Donna and pacify her that this entire FBI was just nonsense and tell her he would be coming home a little early to fix dinner for her and the kids so she could relax.

Matt then activated his resin and finished the fuel tank.

Agent Ruby, however, made good on his promise to never give up and never quit. He did not go back to Matt's shop but he became a presence on the docks of Destin, flashing his badge around, asking questions about Captain Matthew Farrell that stirred up chum and spread gossip faster than the red tide on the shores of the Gulf of Mexico.

'Where is Captain Hight?' Ruby flashed his badge at a deckhand and was told the Captain was in South Fla. With his badge and bad attitude on full display Ruby demanded to see the logbook of the charter vessel, 'I need to see the logbook'

It never occurred to the frightened deckhand to ask for a warrant from the FBI agent. He just went to the wheelhouse, got the logbook and handed it over.

Captain Hight's logbook contained an entry that on a certain date he had built an artificial reef with Matt Farrell. Agent Ruby smiled and wrote down the dates in his ever present yellow legal pad. He also took pictures of the logbook pages, the boat and finally snapped a picture of the shaking deckhand. He handed the young man a card and told him, 'Make sure Captain Hight calls me immediately on his return.'

He left without another word, knowing the young man would run to AJ's and tell everyone what had just happened because of his Captain's involvement with Captain Matthew Farrell.' He smiled a thin smile. He already knew from his endless snooping and dock gossip that Captain Hight and Captain Farrell had history that should help him immensely once he got the sordid details.

Captain Hight was an idiot captain that Matt no longer worked with after an episode that got a port order put against the Reef Runner. This had caused Matt a fair amount of grief with the law. Captain Hight wanted some fishing reefs made and had brought Matt some dumpsters to sink for the reefs. Then Captain Hight got so drunk he did not show up to haul the dumpsters off the boat for his reefs. Matt threatened him with keeping his money for his time and trouble and brought the dumpsters back to the dock to sell to someone else for a reef. Once back in his slip in the harbor Matt got slapped with a Captain of the Port Order when his cargo was inspected.

Matt informed Captain Hight that he needed to sober up and get the dumpsters off the Reef Runner before he recovered from his hangover, 'I don't care how you do it get 'em off my boat. They need to disappear.'

The next day, Matt was working in the boatyard and got a phone call from the 18th floor of the Destin Yacht Club. It was the Captain of the Summer Escape who said, 'Hey I just thought you might want to know there is a big green dumpster in the water right beside your boat.'

Matt stopped rolling gel coat, 'What? You have to be kidding me....'

Matt passed off on the gel coat to Charles and immediately went down and sure enough some idiot had dragged the dumpster off the Reef Runner in the harbor right beside the boat. Matt thought fast on his feet and ran his anchor chain through the door of the dumpster and pulled the Reef Runner on top of the dumpster so the lunch crowd at Harry T's wouldn't look down and see this huge dumpster in the water and start calling the Marine Patrol.

Later that night, Matt got a friend with a crane to slip down to the Harbor after the bars and restaurants had closed and lifted the dumpster out of the water and onto a truck where it finally disappeared.

Matt then filed in small claims court for all his related expenses and had Hight served during happy hour at the Captains table of AJ's.

Agent Ruby keep at it, collecting little nuggets and finding anyone who would talk about Captain Farrell or reef building. Matt recovered his money on this fiasco, but Captain Hight was now Captain Hook towards Matt. Anytime he got the opportunity to badmouth Matt he took it.

Bo Calhoun keep watch on the harbor and decided his best course of action would be to keep Regina Bates happy. The Coast Guard got a call every time the Reef Runner left the docks with a load of reef building material.

An entire sun baked summer slid by, filled with tourists, fishing charters and reef building. With the Rodeo coming up in October Matt was busy. He was using chicken cages now to make large reefs. The open weave of the metal made it faster for small creatures to attach and encrust the metal, turning the metal into a thing of beauty filled with happy grouper and snapper.

Charles showed up at the Reef Runner reeking of rum and panic. 'Cap, I got served, look!'

Charles had been subpoenaed by the United States Government thanks to Agent Ruby to come to Federal Court in Pensacola to testify before the grand jury.

Matt took the blue envelope from Charles shaking hands and opened and read it. He sighed. He had a very brief flash to Agent Ruby's infuriated red face as he snarled that he would not give up and he would be back. Matt folded the envelope back up and handed it back to Charles. 'Don't lose that my man.'

Matt put his hand on Charles shoulder, Charles could not have looked more miserable than if you told him AJ's had run out of rum and women. 'Charles, listen to me man, just tell the truth. I'm the Captain and I'm responsible 100%. But please be careful to not let them put words in your mouth, if you don't know say I don't know, but tell the truth. It's going to be okay. Truth always wins out, Charles, remember that, OK?'

Charles came back from his date with the grand jury in Pensacola and told Matt that the FBI guy was there, Captain Hight was there too. Charles told Matt that they called him in and asked him about the reefs and the fiasco with Captain Hight. Charles said  he told them everyone in Destin had been building fishing reefs for 50 years, you could come down to the docks in Destin during the winter and the entire dock would be covered with cars, washing machines and it's not like Captain Farrell was the first person ever to do this.

The grand jury refused to issue Agent Ruby his warrant for reef building. Ruby's fury at the judgment shot his blood pressure so high he almost passed out. He had to loosen his tie and take many deep breaths before he could stand up and leave the courtroom.

# Chapter 8



*DESTIN TO PENSACOLA, FLORIDA*

It is said that sharks can smell one drop of blood in the water from a mile away. This is an exaggeration of the sharks sense of smell, but once blood is detected in the water by a sharks superb olfactory senses they will home in on the direction the blood came from then circle their potential victim, moving in for the kill on a tasty target.

Agent Ruby hung up the phone. He reached into his ever-present briefcase and dry swallowed five Tylenols.

He had just taken a serious ass chewing from a ranking member of the Senate Judiciary Committee over the lack of evidence for the grand jury to issue an indictment on Captain Matthew Farrell. He would not take another one. As instructed, he now placed a call to the Coast Guard Office in New Orleans and requested copy of the Captain's merchant mariner license filings. He also placed a call to John Barber, the special investigator with the Coast Guard and set up a meeting to discuss Mr. Barber's previous investigation of Matthew Farrell.

Agent Ruby discovered to his delight that Captain Farrell had hit some snags in getting his Captain's license. And had in fact, had to go to New Orleans to speak with the Director, Dr. Paul, related to his documented sea time prior to passing the merchant mariner exam.

A disgruntled and disgraced deckhand, and former Captain that Matt had previously worked with on a fishing charter had sent the examination office a certified and notarized letter that Matt had falsified his sea time on his application. Matt was then summoned to New Orleans with the logbooks from the Reef Runner and the Class Act to give an account of himself, the logbooks and this very serious allegation.

In Dr. Paul's office Matt laid out the story of how he had hired this Captain to sleep in the V-berth of the Class Act, being the 'captain' on board, providing legal coverage with his license while Matt ran the charters, and kept the log book up to date, getting credit for the sea time. When Matt discovered this so-called Captain was bringing hookers to the boat during the day when no charters were scheduled, Matt fired him. The Class Act was owned by a judge who lived in Tennessee and loved to come to Destin to fish and did not need or want hookers doing business on his yacht. With his documented sea time from his own vessel, the Reef Runner, Matt did not really need the extra hours documented on the Class Act to obtain his license. So therefore, what motivation did he have to falsify it?

Dr. Paul examined the logbooks of both vessels, agreed with Matt and told him to continue his testing process.

But the certified letter remained in Matt's file and had raised questions even after Dr. Paul cleared Matt for testing and the license was issued.

After speaking with John Barber and obtaining the copy of all the files, including the letter and a statement from the Captain insisting that Matt did not have the sea hours documented on the Class Act Agent Ruby smiled. He had his blood in the water and was homing in for the kill.

Captain Matt was in the fiberglass shop on Mountain Dr. he had the cash box out on his desk and was cleaning snorkeling equipment. A friend of his had convinced him that putting picnic tables on the Reef Runner with umbrella's and taking tourists snorkeling would be a great new way for him to make money without the constant Coast Guard harassment. Matt was getting tired of putting on a show for the condo queens with their six hundred-dollar telescopes on Holiday Isle as the Coast Guard practiced their Miami Vice showboating moves chasing him down to inspect his reef building material. Matt could not decide if these condo queens hated fisherman or were really concerned for the environment, but either way they were wrong.

Just last week he and Charles had spent two days removing the engines, transmissions, batteries and gas tanks from six Volkswagen bugs. Experience had taught Matt that the Volkswagen mysteriously produced more fish than any other type car he used as reef building material. Other skippers insisted it was the rounded shape but Matt knowing that German's built cars to last, believed it was the primer. Either way six of these coveted cars were headed out into the gulf to make a fine new home for a grouper family along with snappers, trigger and the little baitfish that would tantalize the amberjack.

As Matt passed by a towering condo and into the pass he thought that if the condo queens knew how much work was put into cleaning this 'junk' and what it turned into, producing thousands of dollars in prime gulf seafood they may lay off blowing up the Coast Guard's phone lines and  show some compassion to a guy just trying to earn a decent living and provide for his family.

After clearing the jetty's the Reef Runner finally started making headway against the incoming tide and as they approached the Sea Buoy Matt yelled to Charles, 'Grab that 4 ought reel and take that lure off it and put a 3 oz wt. and drop it back about a hundred yards!'

'What kind of fish you gonna catch with no hook Cap?' Charles yelled back.

Captain Matt laughed, 'a coast guard blue runner!'

'Charles frowned and scanned the area behind them, 'I don't see no Coast Guard today Cap?'

'That's why they call it fishing Charles, I got a feeling we are gonna get a bite here soon.'

Sure enough, about a mile from the sea buoy, and still highly visible from the condo's lining the shore Matt spotted something orange out of the stern window of the wheelhouse. Picking up his binoculars his suspicion was confirmed. Destin's finest was in hot pursuit coming under the Destin Bridge into the pass.

The 32-foot pursuit boat running wide open closed the gap between them and the Reef Runner with siren wide open and enough blue lights to turn the pass into a disco.

Matt looked back and noticed a helmsman on the front of the vessel holding on to the bow line and bouncing up and down like a cowboy on a bucking bull. He started laughing uproariously and Charles just gaped.

'He looks like George Washington crossing the Delaware, Charles!' Matt could not stop laughing. Just then the crewman at the wheel decided to add a touch of flare to the show and cut hard from starboard to port throwing spray into the air and looking very cool, but his cool maneuver jerked George Washington around, almost tossing him overboard and his uniform hat went flying. Matt was laughing hysterically hoping all telescopes were aimed at this fiasco and Charles almost choked on his Copenhagen.

The coast guard vessel powered down and did a tight circle to retrieve the hat before resuming pursuit of the Reef Runner.

As the vessel pulled up beside him, Matt stopped laughing. Over the past year he had been questioned, stopped, boarded and inspected so many times he was losing patience with the process. 'Charles pull that line in before they get it tangled in their prop.'

He then left the wheelhouse to face the Coast Guard. As usual the conversation did not go well. After about fifteen minutes, Matt said, 'look boys, just handcuff me and take me in. I have had enough of this, and I want to go in front of a judge to rule on this.'

The Coast Guard guys just gaped at him. They looked at each other and one shrugged. Then the helmsman picked up the mike and said, 'Chief? He wants us to arrest him and take him in front of a judge?'

Everyone just stood there till over the radio the Chief snarled, 'Just tell him to go on! Dammit!'

Matt shook his head to clear his thoughts from the Coast Guard and wiped down the last mask with his bleach solution. Yes, he thought, taking a group of tourists out to the jetties to look at fish was not as profitable, but a lot more peaceful.

Matt's peace was shattered as a black crown Victoria screeched to stop in front of Matt's open shop door. Before the sandy dust could settle Agent Ruby got out of the driver's side and a huge black man the size of an NFL linebacker got out of the passenger side. Agent Ruby had a huge smile on his face as he strode into the shop towards Matt.

Matt had just enough time to admire his huge teeth and note that he had never seen Agent Ruby's teeth before... 'Matthew Farrell, you are under arrest for obtaining a merchant mariner's license under false pretenses.'

Agent Ruby had not slowed down his race-walking stride towards Matt as he spoke. He pulled out handcuffs from under his suit jacket and they jingled as he flipped them up into his palm.

'Well, here we go...' thought Matt, 'whatever game this guy is playing is now to the last hand.'

The enormous black agent stood in the doorway with his arms folded across his chest. He did not say a word or move to enter the shop.

A short man in cut offs ran into Matt's shop with a look of complete confusion on his face.

'Tim!' Matt said, 'Look man, I'm going to Pensacola with the FBI and I need you to call Charles for me. Tell him I can't run the snorkeling trip today. Tell him to call a Captain, run the trip, do the best he can and make sure he has this cash box and keys.' Matt slid the box across his desk and tossed Tim a set of keys. Tim nodded and grabbed the box, shooting a terrified look at Ruby as he ran back out the door past the linebacker in a suit. Agent Ruby held out the handcuffs to Matt. Matt stuck out his arms in front of his body while deciding to call the linebacker Stone face.

The huge man still had not said a word or moved a muscle. Ruby grabbed Matt's arm and handcuffed him in the front, then grabbing his upper left arm hard enough to leave bruises started leading him towards the crown Vic.

Stone face finally moved and shut the shop door, then walked towards the crown Vic and opened the back door, Ruby steered Matt towards the back and shoved him towards the back.

Matt got in and sat down in the comfortable large seat. He immediately had to slide over towards the passenger side as Agent Ruby got in the back right beside him and continued to grin his humorless yet satisfied grin.

He leaned towards Matt and Matt shrank back in the seat. 'You know,' Matt said pleasantly, 'I don't watch a lot of TV, but on TV people get read their Miranda rights? Did you forget to do that?' He smiled.

Ruby's smile disintegrated into a snarl.

Matt continued to smile pleasantly at him, thinking, 'Now that is a normal Ruby look!'

Ruby leaned back, rolling his eyes and started mumbling, 'You have the right to remain silent...if you give up the right to remain silent anything you say may be used against you in a court of law...'

Matt was not really listening to his rights. He knew that right here, right now with stainless steel cuffs on his wrists, sitting in the back of an unmarked cop car with a very happy FBI Agent, he had no rights.

But knowing he had the law on his side and knowing he had done nothing wrong Matt felt rather chatty. After all he and Agent Ruby were about to ride side by side for an hour to the Pensacola Federal Courthouse. At least Donna thought he was going out on his snorkeling trip so it would be a while before she knew anything and started to panic. Hopefully Matt would be able to call her once they got to Pensacola and she would at least hear about this from him and he could tell her it was all going to be okay.

Matt and Ruby spoke freely about artificial reef building. The craziness in Destin surrounding fishing, drinking, and the beauty of the Gulf of Mexico. Matt told Ruby that people had been coming up with ways to gather fish in the gulf for 50 years building 'reefs' out of everything from old Christmas trees to chicken cages to wrecked cars. What he was doing now was simply an old fisherman tricks on a much larger scale but following the rules set forth by the Army Corp of Engineers, the Marpol Act and all the other government agencies that had their fingers in the water.

Ruby just kept smiling and let Matt prattle on.

Matt was surprised the ride to Pensacola flew by. He had just got done explaining to Ruby how the Japanese had increased seafood production by building huge artificial reefs and establishing sensible quota's and bag limits.

Stone face had not participated or even moved his head till they pulled in front of the courthouse.

He pulled right in front of the steps and slammed on the brakes. Matt's head snapped forward and he looked at the huge stone and marble edifice of justice. Stone face got out of the driver's side of the Crown Vic and let Agent Ruby out of the back-driver's side.

Instead of helping the handcuffed Captain get out of the car, Ruby went around and popped the trunk.

Stone Face finally broke his silence, 'Do you need assistance to get out?'

Matt shook his head and scooted to the edge of the seat and was blinded by the bright Florida sunlight. Stone face grabbed Matt's bicep. He propelled Matt toward Agent Ruby who was looking into the trunk of the Crown Vic and reaching in. Matt followed his eyes and in the trunk of the car was a huge reel to reel recorder that was running, and Agent Ruby was fiddling with. Agent Ruby was switching the machine off and stood up and shot Matt his huge toothy grin.

Matt reminded himself that he had operated within the law, with a legal permit and he had nothing to worry about. He flashed Agent Ruby a big smile of his own.

Agent Ruby's happiness as he marched Matt into the cavernous courthouse was infectious. Matt actually felt relieved and happy for him that whatever this grudge he had was finally taken care of. Then they were stopped in the hallway by a US Marshall.

'Do you have a service weapon?' The Marshall addressed Agent Ruby.

'Of course, I do! I am an FBI Agent.' Snapped Ruby, his smile suddenly gone.

'I don't care who you are, you are not carrying a weapon into this courthouse!' Agent Ruby seemed to shrink in Matt's eyes as he reluctantly handed over his gun to the Marshalls. Agent Ruby tightened his grip on Matt's bicep and steered him towards a stairwell headed down. Matt still feeling the relief and now partial hysteria said, 'Well, an FBI agent without a gun is like a Captain without his Loran numbers!'

There was no return of Agent Ruby's smile or good cheer.

At the bottom of the stairwell Matt found himself in the booking department being turned over to the booking officer. Agent Ruby handed him a sheaf of paperwork and with one humorless grin at Matt was gone.

Matt just stood there realizing he was still wearing the handcuffs and figured he better just stand still and be polite. The booking officer looked confused rifling through the paperwork Ruby had handed him before disappearing.

The booking officer started scratching his head around where his hair line was receding, he looked at Matt and said, 'Why don't you sit right there?' waving at a bench against the wall. Matt sat down and kept watching the officer who appeared more confused and frustrated by the minute.

The booking officer started typing furiously into a computer, frowned again and looked over at Matt. He opened his mouth, shut it. Looked at the computer screen again and finally said, 'Look man, what did you do?'

Matt smiled, 'I built fishing reefs in the Gulf of Mexico.'

The officer frowned, 'I am sorry. I can't find anything in here to charge you on. This does not make any sense. I've got murder, arson, bank robbery, grand larceny.... I don't even have a space to put in this merchant mariners license business.' The officer picked up a phone and mumbled at someone, put the phone down and said, 'I'm sorry this is taking so long.'

Matt continued to smile, 'No problem, I'm enjoying the air conditioning.'

The officer mumbled to person on the phone must have told the booking officer something and finally Matt was officially charged, un handcuffed, fingerprinted and put in a cell with another man. It did not take Matt long to figure out that he was in a cell with the only other completely innocent person in this building.

His new roommate was cordial enough and they shared bologna and cheese sandwiches for lunch.

After lunch another office came to escort Matt to a telephone.

Matt thought quickly, Donna would be setting out snacks for after school and preparing for whatever activity happened this evening and dinner. If he called her, she would get hysterical then have to find a babysitter and drive to Pensacola. That could take hours. No, his best bet to get out of here and home by dinner so he could calmly tell Donna that this was no big deal was to call a friend from church who was a practicing criminal attorney.

The call was placed, and Matt's friend instructed him to sit tight, he had a partner in Pensacola he would send over immediately to represent Matt at his first appearance.

About thirty minutes later Matt was escorted up to a court room where he met the attorney and they were sent in front of a female judge. She was reading the official booking documents and her eyebrows were creeping north on her forehead as her eyes got wide. She composed her face quickly and looked at Matt like he was a very interesting exhibit in some strange museum.

The door to the right of the judge's bench swung open and the United States attorney marched in, glaring at Matt on her way to the prosecutors table.

'No matter what she says, do not interrupt or speak out.' Matt's new attorney friend hissed in his ear.

Matt nodded and continued to smile pleasantly.

Melinda Mayflower introduced herself all around and began her opening monologue. Matt bit his tongue when he almost started laughing at her when she was waving her arms in circles explaining to the judge that Matt had built FISHING REEFS in the Gulf of Mexico AND did it on a Merchant Mariners License that had been obtained under FALSE PRETENSES! She paced up and down in front of the tables and passionately laid out her case that Matt was one of the FBI's most wanted criminals and had finally been brought to this hallowed hall of justice and JUSTICE must be served.

Matt noted that the Judge did not seem amused or even understanding of the seriousness of the charges laid out on him, America's Most Wanted Reef Building Criminal.

After a blessed moment of silence, the Judge said, 'Mr. Farrell, do you have any firearms in your possession?'

'Yes, your Honor, I have some hunting rifles and pistols, family heirlooms handed down by my grandfather.'

The Judge looked at the federal attorney and said, 'How does the state feel about Mr. Farrell's firearms?'

Ms. Mayflower with a pained expression on her face said, 'Your Honor the state requests that Mr. Farrell transfer them out of his possession during these proceedings, after all this is a very serious matter.'

The judge looked at this woman like she was insane but sighed and turned to Matt. 'Mr. Farrell do you have someone you could transfer possession to during these 'proceedings" She dragged out the word proceedings and shot Ms. Mayflower a glare.

Matt replied, 'Yes your Honor, I can take them a friend's house or whatever you require.'

'Done' the judge banged her gavel, 'Can you bond yourself out Mr. Farrell?'

'Yes, your Honor, I can.'

'Are there any more requests from the government?' The judge looked at Ms. Mayflower.

'No, your Honor. Not at this time.'

The gavel banged again. Twenty minutes and two hundred dollars later Matt was back outside in the Florida sunshine looking for a ride back to Destin.

# Chapter 9



*DESTIN, FLORIDA*

Matt got home in time for dinner. Donna was in a good mood, so he knew she had not heard any local gossip and had no idea he had been sidetracked to the Federal Courthouse in Pensacola today. He was relieved.

He led the family in prayer, and they dove into to Donna's spaghetti feast. He crunched on garlic bread and noticed that Donna had overloaded the boy's plates. No way they would be able to eat what Mamma had piled on their plates. He laughed at Abby stuffing her face and ending up with red sauce all over her. Donna still kept long terry cloth bibs for the Princess of the Family. For royalty, she had the table manners of a piglet, not a princess. After the family had made somewhat of a dent in the huge bowl of pasta, Matt directed the boys to clean the table.

'Honey just let Abby sit there, she needs to go directly to the bath after this.' Donna and Matt looked at the little girl with a tomato red face and shared a laugh. Abby even had spaghetti sauce in her blonde curls.

'Yes ma'am, I think you are correct in that assessment. You take her to the tub; the boys and I will clean up in here.' Matt said, smiling at Donna.

'You're sure? I know you have had a long day?'

Matt thought, 'you have no idea my love, but your about to find out.'

He smiled at his wife and reached out and gave her hair a playful tug. 'You go ahead and take her. We've got this, and I'll toss the boys in the tub when we are done.'

Donna looked surprised and relieved. She scooped up Abigail and carrying the sauce covered toddler at arm's length, headed towards the bathroom. Matt and the boys cleared the table and Matt sent them to their bathroom to get cleaned up while he washed the dishes.

About an hour later Abby was safely tucked into her bed, her stuffed lamb got to ride the pillow tonight. 'That's appropriate,' thought Matt, 'I feel like a lamb stuffed for slaughter myself right about now.' He kissed the sleepy little girl and closed her door.

He stopped in the boy's room and said prayers with Caleb and Joshua then tucked them in too. He wondered briefly when his boys would stop letting him tuck them in. He was just glad it was not tonight. Matt gave his son's a quick kiss on the forehead and left to go find Donna.

Donna had plopped down in her chair in the den.

Matt took her hand, 'Let's go outside, it's nice out.' He led Donna out the sliding glass door to sit by the pool.

'It's beautiful and the kids are in bed! This is heaven!' she smiled at him.

Matt started talking and Donna's smile quickly faded. The relentless pressure was taking its toll on Matt and now Donna's worst fears had now manifested into reality.

'Donna, I don't know what is going on.' Matt said to his quietly crying wife. 'All I can tell you is that the harassment by the Coast Guard has been a lot more intense than usual. And now this FBI guy...'

'Matt, that was almost a year ago he came by here. He's been snooping around this entire time? It's like he is out to get you or something evil like that.' Donna grabbed another tissue and blew her nose.

'I know babe, it does seem like that. But I don't know why. And he got nowhere with trying to nail me on reef building, so now he has dragged up the sea time on my license. It seems personal with this guy. But it all started with his insistence that I had no legal right to build reefs. Somehow this is about the reefs.'

'What are we going to do?' Donna started crying again. 'What if they convict you of something?'

'Donna, they arrested me on a bogus charge. You know I have the sea time and you know I was cleared by Dr. Paul to test for my license. I feel like reef building is coming to a quick end, the handwriting is on the wall.  It's less money to run snorkeling trips than building reefs but the hours are better for our family... and I don't have the Coast Guard chasing me down over tourists getting sunburned on deck.'

Donna tried to smile.

'I'm going to go talk to that big shot attorney from church and get his advice on this, ok? I need you to trust me and this is all going to be okay?'

Matt grabbed Donna's arms and pulled her into his lap. She wound her arms around his neck and Matt held her tightly until she stopped shaking.

The next morning Donna was her usual bright self as she got the kids up and ready for school. She had even made a hot breakfast for the family and the kitchen was a mess of bacon grease and flour.

Donna took the kids to school and Matt headed to Fort Walton Beach to go see the attorney from church.

Dan Drake was friends with a member of Matt's church that Matt had built a huge fishing reef for. Matt knew this attorney had been fishing on that reef several times with their mutual friend. Matt had also seen Dan at church about three weeks ago when he came to see one of his grandson's get baptized.

Matt was feeling positive that the secretary had set the appointment without asking what this was about or how Matt knew Mr. Drake. He was hoping that Drake remembered him from their brief encounters and would agree to help him out with this mess.

Matt was not put off by the luxurious atmosphere of Drake's office.

He knew you have to be very successful to afford an office like this.

He sat in the overstuffed leather chair and wondered how much the attractive secretary made. Her shoes looked even more expensive than her crisp navy suit.

'Mr. Farrell? Mr. Drake will see you now.' The attractive brunette led him to a closed office door and smiled.

Matt returned her smile and opened the door and went in. The first thing he saw in the huge office was the wall of baseball memorabilia. All signed and in cases. Matt wanted to walk to the wall and examine these treasures but the man behind the desk stood up and said, 'Matt! Good to see you! What in the world can I help you with?'

Matt walked towards the desk and shook hands with the feared attorney. 'Dan, thank you for your time today. I appreciate you man.'

'Not a problem. I have spent many happy hours fishing thanks to you. Now what's your problem?'

'You don't waste any time, do you?' Matt laughed, 'okay, here goes...'

Matt retraced the entire story for the attorney, starting with the dramatic increase in Coast Guard harassment, the arrival of Agent Ruby, the failed indictment for artificial reef building and now the arrest for obtaining his merchant mariners license under false pretenses.

Dan listened and when Matt was done, he just stared at him.

Finally, Dan stood up and turned his back on Matt staring out the window that overlooked the Sound.

Matt swallowed and waited.

Dan turned around and said, 'this is not what you want to hear but I'm not going to lie or sugarcoat it for you Matt. This sounds like they are trying to break you. These guys know exactly how much I charge by the hour and if you can even retain me, they are going to have us burning up the road between here and the Pensacola Federal Building. If I was you, I would just bend over, take it and ask them to please tell me when they are finished. They want to break you mentally and financially. Don't take it personally, it's just a government procedure.'

Dan continued, in spite of Matt's shocked expression. 'My best advice to you is to plead indigent and ask for a public defender. If you can get Daniel Keys, he is the best over there. Once the feds realize they are fighting with their own money they will flush you through the system as quickly as they can. Again, I know that is not what you want me to say but it's the truth.'

Matt was uncharacteristically quiet. He looked at the floor. He felt the truth of Dan Drake's words. Nothing else made sense. Someone somewhere was on a mission to change the coastal culture and somehow, he had gotten himself in the crosshairs. The Coast Guard harassment, the FBI investigating artificial reef building. Something stunk, badly, and it didn't smell like fresh fish to Matt. He wondered if Regina Bates had something to do with this mess. Matt felt that had to be an accurate assessment. That little wet hen of a woman was not happy unless she was causing trouble for someone else. But was she the instigator or just a tool? Matt decided it did not matter. His reef building days were over, he knew it in his heart now.

Matt stood up and faced Dan Drake, he strode to the man by the window who was just watching him silently.

'Dan, you barely know me, but you made time for me today. And you gave me the situation truthfully. I want you to know how much I appreciate you for that.' Matt stuck his hand out and the two men shared a firm handshake.

'Anytime. Now you see if you can get Daniel Keys assigned to your indigent ass and get yourself out of this mess!' Dan replied. 'Let me know what happens?'

'Yes sir! Will do' Matt saluted the attorney and walked out of his office.

He decided to run back home and see what Donna was doing. His best bet for staying in 'happy wife territory' was to keep Donna in the loop about this mess that had dropped into their perfect little cul-de-sac life.

Donna was doing laundry and gave Matt a huge hug when he told her to grab her purse, he was taking her to lunch. Over their favorite fried fish baskets at Dewey Destin's on the Bay he told her about the meeting with Dan Drake and that he was going to run to Pensacola in the AM and meet with the public defender Drake had recommended.

To Matt's great relief, Donna had progressed emotionally from hysteria to anger. 'Matt, this is complete BS! You went to New Orleans and straightened out all that sea time mess with Dr. Paul years ago! Why are they harassing us?'

'My love, I have no idea. I have a feeling it's got something to do with that crazy woman over at the Department of Natural Resources. I didn't go easy on her when her nutjob ideas were going to tie a noose around the neck of everyone in this town who has made a living fishing for generations. I think Dan Drake is correct that I managed to really tick someone off and she is the only one I can think of.'

Matt and Donna held hands and looked out over the water at Crab Island. 'Donna, I am going to focus on the snorkeling trips and get out of reef building. Whatever the situation is, the heat on us seems to be coming from that and we don't need to do that to make a decent living.'

'I trust you Matt.' Donna squeezed his hand and kissed his cheek. 'I know it will be okay, you can fix anything.'

She flashed Matt the smile that had made him marry her in the first place and Matt knew that come hell, highwater or Regina Bates he was going to fix this for his family.

Matt spent some extra time on his knees that night and in the morning, he left for Pensacola.

His first stop was to the clerk's office to get the indigent form and fill it out. Then he asked to speak with Mr. Keys.

Mr. Keys entire office was smaller than Dan Drake's waiting room and there was not a leather chair in sight. Matt was a little concerned that the plastic chair might break out from under him when he sat in it.

Mr. Keys sat quietly as Matt went through the entire maniacal episode in Destin with him as he had with Drake. He barely glanced at the file Matt had retrieved outlining the Government's case against him.

Key's realized before Matt got a quarter into the story that there was more to this than met the eye. And the government attorneys were not about to lose this case. They had a total of almost two years invested at this point in trying to 'get' Captain Matthew Farrell and had finally secured an indictment with a bogus charge! Whatever this was really about, it was a big fat looser and Mr. Keys did not like to lose.

Even as a public defender he had a reputation to uphold.

So again, Matt finished his unbelievable tale and sat in silence in an attorney's office.

'Mr. Farrell, you told me you spoke with Dan Drake and he recommended me to you?'

'Yes sir, he did.' Matt replied.

'And you told him all this exactly as you relayed the story to me?'

'Yes, I did, and I told you what he advised me to do.'

'Mr. Farrell, I have to agree with Mr. Drake. There is something, and I can't imagine what, but something else at play here. I agree with Mr. Drake 110%, your best bet is to plead guilty, plead out, bend over, take whatever it is and don't ask for a kiss when it's over. This case is a looser. The government is not going to lose, you are. So, do whatever it is they want and make it easier on yourself and your family. I can't help you win this because this case is not a winner. But let's see what the government comes up with as far as a plea deal, are you willing to do that?'

Matt was stunned. 'Who said all attorneys were liars?' he wondered. 'I've met two in two days and they don't want a dime, and both have told me a solid truth.'

Matt stood up. 'Thank you, sir, I appreciate your time to see me and the fact that you are being so honest with me. But I do not want to plead guilty to something I did not do wrong. It's the principle of the thing!'

The attorney looked long and hard at Matt. 'I understand that, I do. But you must understand that you are going up against the United States Government. I don't know who you have pissed off, but you are not winning this case. You need to talk about your future with your wife and let me know what you are willing to do. Maybe we can make this loss a little less painful.'

Matt nodded, shook Mr. Keyes hand and again thanked him for his time and assured him he would be in touch very soon.

Matt was lost in thought on his long drive home from Pensacola. This had not gone as planned but he knew that both attorneys were telling him the truth.

About five miles east of Navarre on highway 98 Matt spotted a huge garage sale and pulled over. He spied a huge bright blue blow up sofa that he just had to check out. To his surprise the sofa was brand new, no holes or patches and had cup holders. The lady had the original box for it too!

Matt could not resist; he could tie this up for a float at Crab Island and the boys and Abby would go nuts over it. He offered the elderly lady running the garage sale five dollars for it and she gave him a toothy grin and yelled, 'Sold!'

She pulled the plug to deflate the sofa and it started to shrink back down to box size. Matt followed her to the table where the cash box was and pulled out his wallet. Beside the cash box were some books and while the woman made change for Matt's twenty, he looked at the books. A shrink-wrapped hardback proclaimed in gold letters,

'YOU and the LAW' a book by Readers Digest.

Matt picked it up. It was a huge, thick hardback that felt like it weighed one hundred pounds. 'Like the weight of my legal troubles right now', Matt thought.

'Would you take a dollar for the book?' he asked.

The old lady didn't even look at it, 'You got it!' she recounted the change and took a dollar back. 'Thanks for stopping!' she said.

Matt smiled at her and walked off with his boxed-up sofa and the Law.

Matt had no trouble deciphering legal codes and regulations. With this book he would study up on Federal Court proceedings and make sure he and Mr. Keys did not get railroaded by the Federal government.

# Chapter 10



*TEXAS*

The crowd at Mellie's Florida Fish House was out of control. The large building had the appearance of a ramshackle wooden fishing shack with a huge porch lined with rocking chairs. Not a chair was empty and the line of waiting patrons stretched out the door across the porch under the hanging bulb lights and into the parking lot. Mellie and her cohorts were in their element talking to the press about the congressional wife's charity endeavors sponsored by their loving husbands to do good work for the communities they served.

Ted stifled a laugh as he recalled how relieved he was that the trucks from Mexico that brought the fish in for tonight's gala charity event had unloaded the precious cargo and were long gone.

Mellie had her arm around one of the lead waitress's and they were explaining to the local news anchor how she was a single mother who had gotten out of a domestic abuse situation. But with no money, no job, no place to live her prospects were dim. Till Mellie Hollis came along and provided a job that included childcare for the workers. Ted had balked at having a 'day care' attached to Mellie's restaurant. But Mellie had stood firm and insisted. Behind the restaurant was a portable building that had two large rooms, one was a playroom/dining room for the kids and the other had bunk beds and some cribs for the little ones when they got tired or their parent had to close and the kids needed to go to bed. The restaurant staff, who needed childcare all took turns being the 'den mom' of the day and no one had to pay for the childcare.

This set up was providing Mellie with dedicated employees who had never had such an opportunity to better themselves, and press coverage that could not be bought.

Ted smiled.

Things just kept getting better and better.

The waitress giving the interview had two kids back in the Kids Hut and was making enough money now to provide her kids with stable housing and mom actually had a decent used car to get them back and forth to their new Nirvana.

As she explained how this had changed three lives for the better, she started to cry, and the camera man focused in on her face as Mellie pulled her in for a hug and held the crying waitress and smiled at the camera.

Ted continued to smile. Damn, he loved Mellie, she was a natural. He hoped no one commented on her new Chanel dress that cost more than this waitress would make in two months.

While watching his wife own the press, Ted missed the arrival of large black Cadillac SUV. Secret Service agents opened the back door and Senator Alex Thibodaux stepped out.

He smiled too. Another man may have seen a successful restaurant and smelled frying fish, but the Senator knew he was looking at a gold mine and smelling money.

He walked up behind Ted with his detail close behind.

'Any chance of getting a bite to eat here tonight? Quite a crowd for the Mellie's event.'

Ted spun around. 'Senator!' He stuck his hand out for a shake, but the older man grabbed his arm and folded the younger man in a quick hug.

Both men stood on the porch, surveying the huge crowd and packed tables in the dining room  and the huge platters of fried fish coming out of the kitchen to happy hungry patrons who felt even better about their over consumption of fried food since it was benefiting the Texas Congressional Wives Charity Event.

'Let's head to the bar Senator'

The men weaved their way through the crowd and headed towards the huge wooden bar. Fish nets, old license plates, and antique fishing gear decorated the bar area light by old Christmas lights.

All the two top bistro tables in the bar area had people standing around with drinks and appetizers waiting on the coveted tables to open up.

Ted and the Senator squeezed in at the bar and the bar tender immediately came up to Ted. 'What will it be Boss?' The bartender gave Ted and the Senator a huge smile.

'I'll take a beer and for you Senator?' Ted turned to Alex with the question hanging in the air.

I'll have a crown on the rocks.' The Senator replied.

'Coming right up!'

The bartender was gone for a nanosecond and back with the drinks.

'Senator, how have you been?' Ted asked after they clinked beer bottle to rocks glass.

'I have been great. My campaign re-election funds are looking very good. I foresee no issues getting re-elected.'

'Excellent news Sir!' Ted smiled. Ted already knew that Senator Thibodaux's campaign was rolling in the money and he knew why.

'And you son? What are your plans? I did not expect you to dive into the restaurant business, I thought your sights were set on Washington?'

'They still are, sir. Or a detour in Austin might be nice. Mellie is so popular now that may be my ticket.' The Senator laughed and turned and shot an appreciative glance at Mellie who was now posing for pictures with customers. 'Never underestimate the power of a former Miss Texas, son, you married well.' The Senator smiled at Ted.

'Now I understand you have another boat in the gulf?'

'Yes sir, thanks to Brad we found a Captain who was willing to go to Mexico and already had governmental contacts. He's running a boat and we are bringing in huge hauls. Tonight, we had two refrigerator trucks unload and re-fill our freezers here. Other restaurants are catching on and buying seafood too.'

He laughed, 'Frozen in blocks fresh from our docks!'

The elder senator leaned into Ted and took an appreciative sip of his whiskey. 'I would go ahead and get another boat going as soon as you can son. Plan to follow that with a distribution warehouse.'

Ted raised his eyebrows in an unspoken question.

'Reef building in the Gulf out of Destin has finally been curtailed, now is the time to get another boat to meet the demand because it won't be domestic commercials who can do it if we can ensure that reef builders are stopped. Ted, I need you to make the phone call needed to ensure this happens.'

Ted smiled and raised his beer bottle towards the senator again. 'Consider it done sir! Consider it done...'


## PENSACOLA, FLORIDA

Regina Bates got to the restaurant and picked a table in the corner shrouded by a huge palmetto palm. The palms gave the restaurant the feel of a café in the Big Easy. She checked her notes then quickly stuffed the index cards back in her pocket as she looked up and saw a large woman with a book satchel type briefcase headed her way.

'Miss Bates?'

'Yes, I am Miss Bates.' The little bird like woman smiled.

'I'm Melinda Mayflower from the US Attorney's office.'

'It's a pleasure to meet you Miss Mayflower' said Regina, sizing her up. Melinda had on a rumpled suit that looked like she got it from a Salvation Army thrift shop and her bare legs were thrust into chunky clogs. The shoulder pads in the suit set off her large frame and made her look like a linebacker. Her only makeup was a streak of orangey blush and matching lipstick.

These two-woman had little in common physically, but in their hatred of men in power they were identical twins.

Wine and appetizers were ordered over the usual chit chat and once a glass of wine had been consumed by each woman Regina leaned in for the initial bite.

'Miss Mayflower, I understand your office just arrested Captain Matthew Farrell on a merchant Mariners violation?'

'Yes, we did.  A grand jury reviewed the evidence against this person and issued our warrant.'

'Well Miss Mayflower, may I call you Melinda?' Regina smiled, 'The Department of Natural Resources, the Department of Environmental Protection, the Corp of Engineers, the Coast Guard and other concerned individuals have been trying to bag Matt Farrell for years on artificial reef construction. With your help we can send a message to every fisherman in the Gulf of Mexico that business as usual is over. Our gulf is too precious to be polluted!'

Regina paused to take a breath and a gulp of pinot grigio. Holding Melinda's gaze, she continued, 'as you may know I hold a position on the Marine Fisheries Commission, and we are reviewing information from studies that show we need strict new bag limits on certain species'

Melinda twisted in her chair; she knew when the government was giving a directive however indirectly. 'What is my part in this?' She took a sip of her wine and picked up a slice of bread.

Regina took another gulp of her wine and said, 'As of this date there is no case law pertaining to artificial reef construction and we need that to change now. Some very powerful people in Washington as well as myself want you to offer this Captain a plea agreement, we must have a guilty verdict on the artificial reef building violation! Offer him whatever you have to, lower it to a misdemeanor but get a guilty verdict! Use the Clean Rivers and Harbor Act of 1899.'

'It sounds like you, yourself are an attorney Miss Bates.' Melinda said as she took another sip of wine and picked up another slice of the bread.

'Trust me, I'm no attorney, but I've been looking forward to this day for years.'

'What if this Captain won't play ball and accept a deal? Do you have a plan B?'

'Oh, he will play, he's a family man. He will gladly swap a felony for a misdemeanor to stay out of prison and take care of his wife and kids... Now let me give you some quick schooling on the detriments of artificial reef construction and the havoc it plays on our ecosystem.'

The waiter arrived with two plates of blacked snapper served over a bed of wild rice and smothered in a spicy crab sauce. Regina attacked her fish like a starving Mako shark. Between bites she prattled on about artificial reefs destroying the ocean floor and its food chain at its most elementary level. By the time the snapper was consumed she had convinced the attorney that artificial reefs were the tool of Armageddon demons determined to bring global warming and death by starvation to the masses of Gulf Coast residents who loved to fish and eat seafood.

As the meal and wine dwindled, Regina smiled as she asked for the check. Mission accomplished! With this conviction of Captain Farrell, the fish heads in Destin would be scared to death to even think of building a reef. With no place for the fish to congregate the catch quotas would sink like an eight-ounce slip lead to the bottom. This would give the appearance of overfishing that Regina wanted. This would allow for the strictest bag limits ever witnessed in the Gulf. With the demand for seafood at an all-time high a select few would make a fortune importing fish from Mexico.

# Chapter 11



*DESTIN, FLORIDA TO PENSACOLA, FLORIDA*

Matt looked at the ties Donna had set out for him choose from. He could not believe that on a beautiful Tuesday morning he was picking out a tie for court instead of piloting the Reef Runner on the gorgeous emerald waters of Destin.

'Well, he consoled himself. 'this was just a formality' With Mr. Keyes compelled by the state to represent an indigent defendant the Government had immediately offered a reduced charge for a guilty plea. It went against everything in Matt, but Donna had cried, begged and then called Matt's sister.

Sandi Farrell had arrived in Destin in her designer suit and huge hair and demanded Matt just 'do the right thing' and end this mess now!

His sister made a passionate argument on behalf of Donna and the children and when she pointed out to Matt that he was booked solid with snorkeling tourists and could not very well run the Reef Runner while in jail, Matt had to concede that the women were right. Not to mention this lined up perfectly with what Dan Drake had advised him.

Matt had agreed to the deal and now he and Donna and Sandi were driving to Pensacola to the federal courthouse to meet Mr. Keyes for the arraignment.

Sandi kept up her usual cheerful chatter and had Donna laughing at her hairdressers' gossip. Matt was content to just drive. But he did not see the white sand dunes and water to his left, nor the green grass and neighborhoods to his right as he headed due west on 98.

He was envisioning driving home from his shop, after dark and blue lights lighting up his rearview mirror. In his horrified mind he pulled over and saw Agent Ruby get out of a black crown Victoria.

Matt recalled the anger the FBI had shown and his dogged pursuit of something, anything to nail Matt on, a guy who was just trying to provide his family a decent life!

In Matt's vision Agent Ruby walked towards his jeep with a bag of white powder in his left hand and his service weapon in his right. Matt's heart was racing, he may have a heart attack before the rogue agent shot him! He heard himself offering to give Ruby the Reef Runner and leave Destin, lock stock and barrel. Ruby just kept grinning his soulless sharks grin as he stood beside Matt and the jeep pointing his service weapon at Matt.

Donna and Sandi were laughing hysterically.

Something about a male hairdresser who was scandalously sleeping with two of his clients who were sisters. He was waiting to see which sister he could convince to leave the rich husbands to be with him and help him open his own salon, but the sisters found out what he was doing, and both dumped him instead of their husbands.

The laughter snapped Matt out of his depressing and frightening reverie and back to the car in the beautiful Florida morning. 'No, no backroad show down with Agent Ruby', he thought. 'I am not going to build reefs anymore. I am pleading guilty and this is over...' But his heart rate said otherwise as the specter of Agent Ruby holding his gun in the dark continued to fill his mind.

He guided the car through Pensacola traffic and pulled into a parking place in front of the Federal Court House. Looking at the stone steps he chewed up two Rolaids and then opened the doors for his wife and sister.

Mr. Keys was waiting for them in the hallway outside the closed courtroom doors. Matt walked up to him with a smile and shook his hand. The attorney greeted Donna and Matt introduced him to Sandi. 'We ready for this?' the attorney said, looking directly at Matt, 'plead out, get out by lunch? That still the plan?'

Matt sighed and looked down. Donna noticeably flinched and Sandi wacked Matt on the back of the arm. Matt looked up and said, 'Yes sir, that is the plan. Plead out and be done with this.'

Keyes looked long and hard at Matt. 'Ladies, if you would go through security Matt and I will be right behind you.'

Sandi grabbed Donna and propelled her towards the bailiff at the metal detectors.

'Matt are you 100%? Because if you are not, I need to know right now.'

'Yes, I am 100% sure this is what I need to do for my family. You and Mr. Drake are right. I can't win this and a plea bargain, so I don't go to jail is a win. I must do this for Donna and the kids, but if it weren't for them? Whoever it is that I have pissed off this badly would need to show themselves and then we could settle this.'

'Okay. I needed to know that before we head in there.'

Just then there was a ruckus from the metal detector area. 'This is a Liz Claiborne Linen SUIT for your information!' Sandi was indignantly telling the bailiff.

'Ma'am I am sorry, but we do not allow shorts in federal court. It is not court attire.' The bailiff responded. Sandi was getting furious; she had set off the metal detectors and had to pull about 200 bobby pins out of her updo that now was not up and they were not going to allow her entrance because she had on a short suit? In Florida?

Sandi's right hand went out with her finger extended and Matt knew the bailiff was about to get a tongue lashing. He stepped forward and grabbed Sandi's arm. 'Sis, please, it's not a big deal. We have to follow the rules. You can wait out here. So can Donna!' he smiled at her.

'NO, I am not!' Sandi snapped, 'I came down here to support you and I am going to do just that!'

Just then another bailiff stepped up and whispered something to the original officer. He had gone and told the judge that the shorts were knee length and part of a suit set and the judge had allowed it.

He turned to Sandi and said, 'Ma'am, we will allow it for today only since your shorts are part of a suit set, but if you return to court you will need appropriate court attire to be permitted entry.'

He held a little dish with Sandi's bobby pins in it and asked her to step through the metal detectors one more time.

The now disheveled Sandi passed through the metal detector this time without incident followed by Donna, Matt and the attorney.

Together the group entered the courtroom.

The peace of knowing he was doing the right thing and that he was innocent had Matt in an unusual state of serenity for a person about to face a Judge in Federal Court. Matt knew he did not want to continue this battle with Agent Ruby. Ruby was a typical Ruby Ridge, Waco suit and black-tie wearing lunatic who would stop at nothing to satisfy his ego. Matt remembered his threat at their first meeting to 'never stop, never give up and I'll be back.' After more than a year of relentless harassment and intimidating the entire docks of Destin, Matt wished he had not laughed at the man now. It was time to throw the guy a bone and get this over with. Matt sat quietly with Daniel Keys at his side and Donna and Sandi behind them as the Judge walked into the courtroom.

'All rise for The Honorable Robert Benson! Court is now is session.' Bellowed the bailiff. A very distinguished looking older man with an air of determination took the bench and stated, 'Everyone may be seated. Good morning.'


THE COURT: All right, if we're ready we have the matter involving Mr. Matthew Farrell?

MR. KEYES: That's correct, Your Honor.

THE COURT: Case 95-03215. Ms. Mayflower tell me what we have.

MS. MAYFLOWER: Your Honor, Mr. Keyes and I have entered

into plea negotiations along with Mr. Farrell and we've agreed Mr. Farrell will plead guilty to an information we're about to file. The information charges misdemeanor violation of the Ocean Dumping Act. In exchange, in coordination with his plea to the information the United States has agreed to file a motion to dismiss the current indictment that is pending in this case. We've also agreed there are no further, there will be no further charges arising out of his captain's license or his dumping activities in federal court in the Northern District of Florida.

Matt took a deep breath and sighed. He could not believe that the FBI and US Attorney had actually fooled the grand jury into believing there was a violation involving his captains license. A false allegation involving a disgruntled deckhand/captain had already been resolved twice during Matt's examination period. Now it seemed that that the examination officer had developed selective amnesia due to an overzealous FBI agent.

THE COURT: All right. So, what we're going to do is you're going to file an information and we're going to dismiss this case.

MS. MAYFLOWER: Yes, Your Honor, I have those documents prepared.

THE COURT: All right. Mr. Keyes, is that the agreed thing you're going to do?

MR. KEYES: Yes, Your Honor, it's our understanding this takes care of the matter of Mr. Farrell in federal court here, that there would be no further charges brought as a result of any involvement in artificial reef building, something to do with his captain's license which related to the initial indictment there, and any statements to the Coast Guard related to reef building or captain's licenses or anything like that. So, it's just our understanding this will settle the matter short of anything new that involves a homicide. I know the government always reserves the right on that.

MS. MAYFLOWER: Certainly, as relates to the Northern

District of Florida. Of course, I can't commit other districts.

MR. KEYES: I understand it's just this district.

MS. MAYFLOWER: That is correct, Your Honor.

THE COURT: Mr. Farrell, is that what you want to do?

THE DEFENDANT: Yes, sir.

THE COURT: Raise your right hand and I'll have the clerk administer the oath.

DEPUTY CLERK: Do you solemnly swear the testimony you are about to give in this proceeding will be the truth, the whole truth, and nothing but the truth, so help you God?

THE DEFENDANT: Yes, I do.

THE COURT: Tell me your full name.

THE DEFENDANT: Matthew Farrell.

THE COURT: How old are you?

THE DEFENDANT: Thirty-seven.

THE COURT: What's your date of birth?

THE DEFENDANT: 6/24/58.

THE COURT: where were you born?

THE DEFENDANT: Excuse me, where?

THE COURT: Where.

THE DEFENDANT: Monroe County, North Carolina.

THE COURT: Did you go to school there?

THE DEFENDANT: Yes, I did.

THE COURT: Did you graduate from high school?

THE DEFENDANT: Yes, I did.

THE COURT: Did you go on to any other education?

THE DEFENDANT: I attended Wingate College a year and a half.

THE COURT: Well, the next few minutes I'm going to be asking you some questions. If you don't understand the question, want me to explain it, let me know and I'll be happy to repeat or explain.

THE DEFENDANT: Yes, sir.

THE COURT: Mr. Keyes, your attorney, is right beside you. If you want to consult him or ask him a question, I'll give you a chance to do that as often as you feel you need to. I also remind you your answers are being given under oath, and that means your answers have to be truthful and complete. You understand that?

THE DEFENDANT: Yes.

THE COURT: If they're not, you understand you could be charged with a separate offense of perjury?

THE DEFENDANT: Yes, I do.

THE COURT: What's your residence address?

THE DEFENDANT: 512 Stallman Avenue in Destin, Florida.

THE COURT: Who else lives there with you?

THE DEFENDANT: My wife and three children.

THE COURT: All right, what's your wife's name?

THE DEFENDANT: Donna.

THE COURT: Have you ever been treated for any kind of mental illness?

THE DEFENDANT: No, sir.

THE COURT: Have you taken any drugs, narcotics, or consumed any alcoholic beverages within the past twenty-four hours?

THE DEFENDANT: No, sir.

THE COURT: Are you taking any kind of prescription medication?

THE DEFENDANT: No, sir.

THE COURT: It's the intent pursuant to this agreement that you have with the government for them to file an information charging you with knowingly transporting a quantity of metal garbage containers known as dumpsters for the purpose of dumping the material into ocean waters in violation of Section 1411(a) (1) and 1415 (w), Title 33, United States Code. You understand what that charge is all about? This is by information. That is a charge brought by the government in lieu of proceeding through the grand jury in a formal indictment. You understand that?

THE DEFENDANT: Yes.

THE COURT: You realize you have the right to have a formal charge brought like this only after the grand jury has considered it?

THE DEFENDANT: Yes, I do.

THE COURT: You can waive that right if you do it knowingly and voluntarily and particularly if done as a part of a plea agreement like this. Is that what you want to do?

THE DEFENDANT: Yes, sir, at this time.

THE COURT: Have you discussed that at this time? Do we have a waiver?

MS. MAYFLOWER: It's a misdemeanor, Your Honor, he's pleading to.

THE COURT: It's a misdemeanor.

MS. MAYFLOWER: Yes, Your Honor.

THE COURT: I forgot that, thank you. With regard to the charge in the information do you understand you have a right to a trial by jury on the charge?

THE DEFENDANT: Yes, I do.

THE COURT: And do you understand you have an absolute right to remain silent?

THE DEFENDANT: Yes, sir.

THE COURT: You realize you have the right to have an attorney represent you?

THE DEFENDANT: Yes, I do.

THE COURT: You realize you have the right to confront and have your attorney cross-examine the government witnesses?

THE DEFENDANT: Yes.

THE COURT: In open court?

THE DEFENDANT: Yes.

THE COURT: You have the right to subpoena witnesses and compel them to testify for you. You understand that?

THE DEFENDANT: Yes, sir.

THE COURT: You have the right to plead not guilty to this charge, and if do you that the burden is entirely the government's to prove you're guilty with proof beyond a reasonable doubt, a very high standard of proof, and you yourself are presumed to be innocent so you don't have to prove anything. You understand that?

THE DEFENDANT: Yes, I do.

Matt could not hold the Judges gaze any longer, his premonition of a mean, angry judge, full of wrath had quickly diminished. It seemed that the judge was practically begging him to plead 'not guilty'. But the specter of Agent Ruby on the dark streets of Destin would not go away.

THE COURT: If you plead guilty each of those rights will have been waived and given up. Do you fully understand that?

THE DEFENDANT: I do.

THE COURT: Knowing that, you're going to plead guilty to this charge?

THE DEFENDANT: Yes, I am.

THE COURT: You fully understand the difference between a guilty and not guilty plea?

THE DEFENDANT: Yes, I do.

THE COURT: There will be no further trial if I accept your guilty plea. You understand that?

THE DEFENDANT: Yes, I do.

THE COURT: You also know you waive any defenses you may have when you plead guilty?

THE DEFENDANT: I understand.

THE COURT: You cannot appeal when you plead guilty. You understand that?

THE DEFENDANT: Yes, sir.

THE COURT: At least the question of guilt or innocence. It's final when I accept your guilty plea so you can't think about it and change your mind later and withdraw the plea. Is that clear?

THE DEFENDANT: I understand.

THE COURT: Do you understand fully what this charge is all about?

THE DEFENDANT: I do.

THE COURT: I'm going to ask Ms. Mayflower to put on the record the facts pertaining to this charge the government is prepared to establish through evidence. After she's finished, I'll ask you a few questions about it. So, listen carefully to what she says.

MS. MAYFLOWER: Your Honor, in approximately 1987 the defendant, Matthew Farrell, built a vessel called the REEF RUNNER for the purpose of running a reef building business in Destin, Florida. Reef building is regulated by the United States Army Corps of Engineers and a permit is necessary by the Corps to legally build a reef. Farrell never obtained a permit to build privately-owned reefs though he was aware of the requirement. Further, much of the material he dumped through the years was prohibited under the Army Corps regulations because of its potential harm to the environment. The defendant built numerous illegal reefs without a permit up to and including September 1993, primarily for commercial fishermen in the Destin area. One reef was built in or about August of 1992 when the defendant dumped a quantity of dumpsters offshore off the Destin coast. The dumpsters were transported from the United States for the purpose of dumping them in ocean waters. They were placed on his boat on shore in Destin and dropped inside twelve miles offshore. The material dumped had not been approved by the Army Corps of Engineers and no permit had been obtained for the dumping.

Matt was seething inside but continued to study the floor. If he looked up, he might catch the judge's eye and start yelling the truth.

He knew the SAJ-50 inside and out and he was getting angry at the picture Ms. Mayflower was painting of him as a trash dumping pirate with no consideration for the environment or law.

THE COURT: All right, let me ask you a question. The statute says this does not mean the construction of any fixed structure or artificial island nor the intentional placement of any device in ocean waters or on or in submerged land beneath such waters for purpose other than disposal when such construction or placement is otherwise regulated by federal or state law.

MS. MAYFLOWER: Yes, Your Honor, there is a provision in the statute that allows for permitted reef building. However, if there is no permit under the statute it is considered simply ocean dumping.

THE COURT: What this really is a nonpermitted artificial reef.

MS. MAYFLOWER: Yes, Your Honor.

THE COURT: And there's no other statute that deals with that other than this one?

MS. MAYFLOWER: Your Honor, there are a few others that have misdemeanor provisions that were considered. The Clean Water Act would have applied to this activity as well. The Rivers and Harbors Act probably would have applied. But there were some other types of legal problems that we were facing with those other two statutes, though we probably could have used them. Both of those contain misdemeanor provisions. As far as environmental crimes and misdemeanors that's about the extent of what would have applied to this particular case. The Rivers and Harbors Act was considered but it was rejected because it contains a thirty-day minimum mandatory jail sentence.

THE COURT: All right.

MS. MAYFLOWER: The Clean Water Act was rejected because the misdemeanor provision is a negligence provision and I believe it might have been a bit of a legal fiction to have informed the court this was negligently dumped when in fact it was knowingly dumped.

THE COURT: All right, this is not an environmental discharge; this is basically a fisherman's aid.

MS. MAYFLOWER: Your Honor, the defendant was building reefs. He was selling coordinates to reefs when he was building the reefs. Unfortunately some of the material that he was using through the years we've been able to show was slightly harmful to the environment, that he wasn't following regulations in terms of the types of materials that were being dumped as well, which was more of a significant problem than failing to get a permit.

THE COURT: All right, Mr. Farrell you understand what she said?

THE DEFENDANT: Basically, to an extent.

THE COURT: All right. Are those facts true?

MR. KEYES: Your Honor, let me just speak for him and he can fill it in if he feels the need. He acknowledges that on August, 1992, he did take dumpsters and put them into the water for the purpose of building an artificial reef, that he did not have a permit from the Corps of Engineers or any other federal or state agency in his name to do that at that time. There is some question we talked about whether he believed he had the authority from the County of Okaloosa to do some artificial reef building back before this time period and around this time period, but there's no question that he did not have a permit in his own name from the Corps of Engineers through the federal rules and procedures and regulations that are required to do this. I think he acknowledges that. I mean there's a lot of extraneous things that are maybe debatable about whether what he put in the water was harmful to the environment. I don't know if that can be said. He never intended to do anything to harm the environment or pollute the waters; it was just to build, you know, reefs for fishermen and fishing activities. And so, I think, you know, there would be some disagreement about whether he actually harmed the environment by what he did here.

THE COURT: Well, if I understand what happened Mr. Farrell got some old dumpsters that apparently were no longer usable, old steel dumpsters.

MR. KEYES: Right.

THE COURT: And put them on a barge or something and took them out and dumped them in the water and marked the location so they would attract fish and all the fishermen would know where they were. Is that what you did, Mr. Farrell?

THE DEFENDANT: Yes, sir, that's exactly right.

THE COURT: You did that without getting a permit when you were supposed to get a permit?

THE DEFENDANT: Yes, sir.

THE COURT: That's what we have?

MS. MAYFLOWER: Yes, sir, Your Honor. The United States is also prepared to prove Mr. Farrell did not have permission from the county to build this type of reef and never had permission to build this type of reef and knew he didn't have permission to build the reef. So, I believe we can prove the intent necessary in this case.

THE COURT: Does it make any difference if it's in state waters or international waters?

MS. MAYFLOWER: Your Honor, we're prepared to prove it happened within twelve miles, which is the jurisdiction for the Ocean Dumping Act, as a matter of fact within three miles, which is the jurisdiction for Clean Waters and Harbors as well.

MR. KEYES: Your Honor, I would add I tried to find any cases that involved this statute and could only find one, a district court case from Delaware, and the issue there was what had to be proven as to knowledge and intent, and this particular court found like a strict liability, they did not have to prove knowingly violating the law or knowing, specifying what they were, but knowingly doing the act. And I could not find any other cases.

THE COURT: I think that's true on almost every environmental statute, that imposes it a criminal penalty, sort of a strict liability, you're supposed to know you're not supposed to do that. The problem I have is I know hundreds and hundreds of people have done this, but that doesn't make it legal. You have to have a permit to do it, Mr. Farrell, you understand that?

THE DEFENDANT: Yes, sir, I had at different times had permission and this particular date in question I didn't have permission at this time.

MS. MAYFLOWER: The United States would disagree with that, Your Honor. He's never had permission to do what he did.

THE COURT: As far as this particular time you as acknowledge you had no right to do it, Mr. Farrell?

THE DEFENDANT: Excuse me?

THE COURT: At the time you did this, which is August of 1992, you didn't have a permit and you didn't have anybody's authority to do that?

THE DEFENDANT: That's correct.

MS. MAYFLOWER: Your Honor, if I may just for the court's information, this statute did turn into a felony on October 31, 1992, became a five-year felony, but we charged in August of '92 which made it a misdemeanor, just for the court's information.

THE COURT: The statute was amended then?

MS. MAYFLOWER: Yes, it was amended effective October 16 of '92 and made a felony

THE COURT: Because the version I have, 1415(b), seems to indicate not more than one year.

MR. KEYES: It's in the supplement.

MS. MAYFLOWER: Yes, it was amended.

THE COURT: So, what is the penalty for this offense?

MS. MAYFLOWER: It is a class C misdemeanor, Your Honor, which gives it a maximum penalty of one-year imprisonment, a one hundred thousand dollar fine, one year of supervised release, twenty-five-dollar special assessment.

THE COURT: One-year imprisonment, fine of one hundred thousand dollars or both?

MS. MAYFLOWER: Correct.

THE COURT: Twenty-five-dollar monetary assessment.

MS. MAYFLOWER: Correct.

THE COURT: If a prison sentence is imposed, up to one-year supervised release.

MS. MAYFLOWER: Correct, Your Honor.

THE COURT: You understand what you're facing, Mr. Farrell?

THE DEFENDANT: I understand that.

THE COURT: You acknowledge you did what you're charged with then in this information?

THE DEFENDANT: Yes, sir.

THE COURT: You understand what supervised release is?

THE DEFENDANT: With a parole officer for example?

THE COURT: It's designed to follow imprisonment, so if you get a prison sentence supervised release is a set of conditions following release from prison. You understand that?

THE DEFENDANT: Yes, sir.

THE COURT: You also realize if you get any prison sentence, parole has been abolished so you will not be.

THE DEFENDANT: I understand there's a range of punishment that is involved.

THE COURT: He can't tell you what the guideline range is going to be, and I can't either right now. Has that been explained to you?

THE DEFENDANT: Yes, sir.

THE COURT: Only after the presentence report has been completed will we know exactly what your sentencing range will be. And I have to impose a sentence within that range unless there are circumstances that may authorize me to go above or below the range. You understand all that?

THE DEFENDANT: Yes, sir.

THE COURT: And an appeal may be made by you and the government, but only on grounds set out by statute in Title 18, United States Code, Section 3742. That grounds, those grounds basically relate to how the sentence is computed and calculated and whether it's within the Constitution and law, you understand that?

THE DEFENDANT: Yes, sir.

THE COURT: Anybody made any other promises to you other than as outlined to me as far as the agreement is concerned?

THE DEFENDANT: I can think of none.

THE COURT: Is that the complete agreement then between you and the government as outlined to me? Procedure operates and possible sentence or punishment that may be imposed under the law. Finally, I find you've made your decision to plead guilty freely and knowingly and voluntarily and you've made that decision with the advice of a lawyer with whom you've indicated your full satisfaction. So, Mr. Farrell, let me ask you, how do you plead to the charge in the information?

THE DEFENDANT: I plead guilty, sir.

THE COURT: I'll accept your guilty plea but defer adjudication of guilt until the time of sentencing, which I'll set for Tuesday December 12, at 8:30 in the morning. Now, Mr. Farrell has been released. Any reason why he can't be continued under the same conditions?

MS. MAYFLOWER: No, Your Honor.

THE COURT: That will be the order of the court then. All right, I think that concludes this matter. At the appropriate time, actually I think we can probably go ahead now he's entered the plea and dismiss the other one. Want to do that?

MS. MAYFLOWER: Yes, Your Honor, I have no problem with that.

THE COURT: This case is dismissed.

# Chapter 12



*DESTIN, FLORIDA*

It was a spectacular sunny day and Matt watched Charles help the tourists board the Reef Runner. They had two full loads for snorkeling trips today and one full trip every day for the rest of the week. Business was very good, and Matt could not have felt better. Only once since starting the snorkeling trips had the coast guard checked him and it was a courtesy check on the life jackets and registration. All was in order and they saluted and left. No more hot pursuits, arguing with flunkies or constantly looking over his shoulder for the blue lights. What he had lost in income he had made up for in peace of mind and actually he had not lost that much income. Donna was happy, the kids were extremely happy, and Matt had to admit, life after reef building was pretty good.

Matt had gone to the Captains table at AJ's about a week ago and heard that Captain Gibson was trying to hire some shrimpers out of Bayou La Batre to build him some new reefs. Matt had to laugh, and he just told the other Captains that he would never so much as say the word R E E F and he was never building another one. The table had gone quiet as the Captains contemplated that announcement, and the reason for it.

Matt turned his attention from his thoughts and the sparkling green waters to face the now sitting passengers aboard the Reef Runner all pasty white or sunburned red depending on long they had been in Destin who were ready to go snorkel and see some fish!

Matt got the nod from Charles that all were aboard, and they were ready to depart. Matt picked up his mic and after a quick prayer of thanks began his speech.

'Good morning passengers aboard the Reef Runner! Good to see you all this fine morning. As your Captain aboard this vessel I am required to give you a safety orientation speech by the United States Coast Guard. This speech is designed to consist of all factors you need to be aware of to be safe in the event of an actual emergency.

So, if you would look to my left over there you will see a closet that reads 'life jackets'. Forty-eight adults and six children's life jackets. Under no circumstances are you to use those life jackets! They cost me $1500! So, don't touch them no matter what goes wrong!' Matt could not suppress a chuckle at the horrified looks on the faces of the mother's on board. But at his chuckle the passengers started laughing along with him. Matt continued his safety speech,

'I know a lot of you watch tv and movies and have seen that line 'women and children first'? Well that only applied in the early 1900's, you gals burned your bra's a while back so out here it's every man or woman for themselves. And I know you have heard that line about the 'Captain goes down with the ship'? That does not apply here either! If you see me or the crew swimming to shore, you are BEHIND and need to swim faster! Now do we have any fireman on board? Oh, the family from Tennessee? You, sir are a fireman? Well first of all thank you for your service as a first responder, secondly if the boat catches fire we are going to need someone with experience, so you are it. The fire extinguishers are bolted down right here by the wheelhouse. But please, let it burn past the ten-grand deductible on my insurance policy before you put it out!'

Matt had the entire crowd laughing along with him now. He finished up, 'Now that guy over there is my deckhand Charles, he's got Dr. Peppers, Mountain Dew and water stashed on board somewhere if you get thirsty. And these two fine fellows here are Caleb and Joshua. They are small but mighty! Caleb is our equipment manager so get your snorkel, mask and fins from him. If you come back to the boat and are finished swimming, please return your equipment to him. Joshua is our produce manager, why do we have a produce manager? Well the fish you want so badly to see absolutely adore eating peas. Joshua has little bags of peas for your fish feeding pleasure for sale for only fifty cents. I'm betting none of you have ever had so much fun for fifty cents. I believe Joshua may be offering a sale today! Yes! Two bags of peas for one dollar! Get yours now!  Now you can call me Captain Zig and I ask you to please stay seated as we pull out of the slip and head out into the beautiful Gulf of Mexico. Parents keep your children seated with you as we pull out, no one puts their hands through the rails, nobody gets hurt, everybody has a good time!  And we thank you for choosing the Reef Runner for your vacation fun today.'

The crowd cheered as the Reef Runner pulled out of the slip and headed out into the emerald waters. Caleb and Joshua were quickly out of peas to sell.

Matt smiled, 'yes life is good. I just have to get this sentencing over with and life will be great!'

The following Tuesday Matt and Donna headed back to Pensacola. Matt had convinced Sandi to stay home with the children this time.

### *PENSACOLA, FLORIDA*
### *FEDERAL COURT HOUSE, OPEN COURT.*
Matt was in wonder that again, he felt serene. And as before the Judge came in and got right down to business.

THE COURT: Pursuant to notice we have sentencing for Matthew Farrell in case 95-3215 so, counsel, if you'll come down with Mr. Farrell. All right let me correct the case number. It's 95-03215. All right, are you ready?

MR. KEYES: Yes, Your Honor.

THE COURT: Matthew Farrell, pursuant to your plea of guilty to the single-count information filed in this case, I hereby adjudge you guilty as charged in the one-count information. Now, before I impose sentence this morning, you'll have an opportunity to speak personally and your attorney will have an opportunity to speak on your behalf concerning anything at all you believe I should know about before I actually impose sentence. Before we get to that let me make sure you've personally gone over the presentence report and read it and discussed it with your attorney. Have you done that?

THE DEFENDANT: Yes, sir.

THE COURT: Do you find any factual errors in the report that have not been corrected?

THE DEFENDANT: It seems to be fine, Your Honor.

MR. KEYES: Your Honor, other than what he mentioned to me and what I might have put in the letter to the probation officer no additional corrections need to be made.

THE COURT: Mr. Keyes, you've got some objections. Let's take those.

MR. KEYES: Your Honor, when we received the presentence report, of course Mr. Farrell had pled guilty to a certain specified incident of August, '92, of placing some dumpsters into the Gulf to construct an artificial reef and I guess pursuant to relevant conduct that particular incident was really not hardly mentioned but we got into other possible incidents and things that may have occurred. And in going over the presentence report we raised some, I guess, issues or disputed some of the statements made about some of these other incidents. I'm not really sure if the court needs to resolve all these things we raised or the court under Rule 32(c) may be able to say it's not going to affect your sentencing decision and not make a finding or resolution of fact on this.

THE COURT: Well, the information simply charges in August 1992, Mr. Farrell without a permit did knowingly transport a quantity of metal garbage containers commonly known as dumpsters for the purpose of dumping them into the international waters. Or navigable waters, at least.

MR. KEYES: That's correct, and of course he's pled guilty to that charge. Now, for purposes of the guidelines I mean there may be some issues. First of all, it's not disputed that Mr. Farrell was involved in reef building and had been so for several years. So, there's no dispute that Mr. Farrell, more than on this one occasion, on his boat took material out and placed them in the Gulf to try to construct a reef. In terms of the guidelines, 201.3 I think is what we're dealing with here. There's an adjustment for ongoing or repetitive or continuous discharge and we haven't objected to that guideline specific offense characteristic being applied. Also, there was an increase for doing so without a permit. Now, we have raised the issues of whether there should be a total of a four-level downward departure and we may need to make some decisions about was there any actual environmental contamination or risk of it by Mr. Farrell's conduct. Our position is that there was not any contamination and there was not any risk based on the conduct he was involved in and we're asking the court to make that four-level departure and I see that as maybe the main issue to address for the sentencing, is whether the court is going to do that or not. So, in terms of some of the allegations about that he had, you know, some automobiles.

THE COURT: You know, every time I deal with these regulations and the statutes on, enacted under the Clean Water Act, and this is apparently, is this part of the Clean Water Act?

MS. MAYFLOWER: No, this is a separate section, Ocean Dumping Act, Your Honor.

THE COURT: Which was enacted in, what, 1972, part of the same thing?

MS. MAYFLOWER: Your Honor, I don't know if I know the enactment date,

THE COURT: Marine Protection, Research and Sanctuaries Act of 1992, looks like. All these have re high-sounding names and certainly are well-intentioned. The problem is they're so broadly drafted you can simply apply them to anything. I mean it says if you put sand or rock in navigable waters you've polluted it. Well, that's absurd, absolutely absurd, technically to apply these strictly, so you have to use a little bit of common sense and reason in trying to apply these. And in this instance what really is the charged offense is the violation of the National Fishing Enhancement Act of 1984, which you've provided me a copy of that act having to do with artificial reefs. And what really is the offense conduct in this case is that Mr. Farrell didn't get a permit as he's required to do to make an artificial fishing reef, which I think everybody realizes artificial fishing reefs are environmentally desirable. Certainly, they attract and promote the growth and protection of fishing resources in the water. As long as they're not navigable hazards and don't have any actual pollutants in them they're desirable and they need to be encouraged instead of discouraged. The problem we've got is that this offense doesn't meet the statutory intent or intended purpose so what we're trying to do is force feed it into that and it's creating some problems.

Matt could not believe the Judge's position on all of this. It seemed the Judge was actually arguing for Matt. Mr. Keyes sucked in a deep breath and leaned over and whispered to him, 'I wish I had the court on my side like this more often!'

THE COURT: My intent is, if we can save time, is I'm going to give him both of the departures in accordance with application notes four and seven because I think they're called for in this case. Does the government want to be heard on that?

MS. MAYFLOWER: On the departures, Your Honor?

THE COURT: Yes.

MS. MAYFLOWER: NO, Your Honor. I do, however, want to put the government's position on the record that, yes, we have a permit violation in this case but, Your Honor, the United States feels it's beyond permit violation in this case, that the materials that Mr. Farrell was using in this particular case and the materials Mr. Farrell was using over a period of years were improper materials to be building reefs with. That is one of the more serious problem. The Army Corps of Engineers, as provided to the court through the probation office with a list of materials, that list of materials sets forth very clearly and very plainly what types of materials are proper for building reefs. And Mr. Farrell did not follow those regulations even though he was made aware of those regulations and made aware of the lists and the proper way to build reefs. The dumpsters are particularly listed in this list of Army Corps information and the proper way to build reefs, and we believe--

THE COURT: Tell me why, tell me why they are particularly listed. Because we're not talking about a fifty-gallon, fifty-five-gallon drum that will float away or drift away; we're talking about something that is, what, I would imagine at least a couple thousand pounds. These things are heavy. And they're not subject to being drifted around with

the currents. They're almost as stable as an anchor when you put them on the bottom. So, what's the basis of this regulation? It has to have a reasonable basis.

MS. MAYFLOWER: Are you talking about dumpsters in particular or the list in general?

THE COURT: Well, dumpsters in particular because that's the offense charged. But the regulation says waste receptacles such as portable dumpsters, garbage transporters, et cetera, and who knows what et cetera means.

MS. MAYFLOWER: Your Honor, I think dumpsters are subject to some amount of buoyancy if not weighted down. I know they are heavy but by virtue of the way they're built they're also hollow and have a tendency to hold air and air pockets and they can on occasion float. I don't think there's any problem with dumpsters that are properly weighted and dumpsters that are properly set in a proper area. There wouldn't be any problems with them. But you have to, there are very few things that don't require some sort of preparation to put in the water, so they do not do harm to the environment.

Matt pulled at his necktie. He felt he was choking and took a slow deep breath. He felt if he closed his eyes, he would open them and see Regina Bates in all her little wet hen fury at the prosecutors table. Had he not heard those exact words from her thin lips? He opened his eyes and decided to focus on the Judge and not the ghosts of arguments past.

THE COURT: And again, this is not a regulation even. I don't know what this is, criteria required by the Corps of Engineers for processing a permit application. I don't think it's even got the formality of a rulemaking proceeding behind it. Does it?

MS. MAYFLOWER: Well, Your Honor, the EPA and Congress has delegated the authority to regulate the permitting of ocean reef building to the Army Corps of Engineers. It's within their power to determine what is appropriate for building reefs and what is not appropriate in order to issue permits.

THE COURT: Subject to a reasonable basis.

MS. MAYFLOWER: Certainly.

THE COURT: The law itself, Congress can enact something that without a reasonable basis that can simply fail to meet the requisite due process standards. I'm not sure, I don't want to get too deep in this.

MS. MAYFLOWER: No, Your Honor.

THE COURT: All I'm saying is that all of this is a very broad area and once you start making some of these things into criminal offenses there are all sorts of weaknesses in the attempts to do this and this is not the first time it's been before me and it continues to be a major problem and nobody seems to pay any attention to doing anything about it. But you can't make a criminal offense out of not getting, of failing to get a permit which is subject to a civil fine under this statute, if that's what you've got.

Daniel Keyes stifled a laugh and started scribbling on a legal pad to regain control. The Judge was defending his client! He almost felt sorry for Ms. Mayflower, then he allowed himself a small smile and decided he did not feel sorry for her at all. He shot Matt a look and wrote on the legal pad, 'do not smile or laugh out loud!'

MS. MAYFLOWER: Well, Your Honor, I feel that as EPA does and I can cite to the court a section of the Federal Register where EPA states that unpermitted reef building constitutes illegal ocean dumping under the act. But again, Your Honor, it is our position that this is, this has gone beyond merely getting a permit.

THE COURT: Well, the problem is we've got so many people really polluting the water, and I live on the water and go out there and see it every day, people dumping plastics and all sorts of contaminants in the water continually and nobody does anything about it. And you have somebody putting something in the water you call a pollutant that isn't actually a pollutant and it's a criminal offense and it is disturbing to me we've turned it upside down instead of punishing those really polluting and instead going after those who are perhaps more visible but who are in the long run enhancing the environment. So that's my basic problem with this.

MS. MAYFLOWER: Your Honor, I believe we are doing something about it. I believe that the deterrent effect of prosecuting individuals who are illegally dumping waste products in the ocean is a deterrent. I believe that it has had even an effect in this particular case. We have, I believe, curbed a lot of the dumping that was occurring in the Destin area because of this prosecution. I respectfully disagree with the court that this is not a pollutant, that we are not dealing with pollutants in this case.

THE COURT: Don't get me wrong, there are things being put in the water as fishing reefs that are pollutants, no question about that, things are going out there that shouldn't be in there. And I think if the permitting process is operating as it should be this shouldn't be a major problem. But I'm not sure that the permitting process is functioning in anything like the way it should be. And I think again we're in a bureaucratic maze that makes it very difficult for anybody to understand what the requirements are and what they are not. So, there's a lot of work that needs to be done. Tell me again, are you going to object to my departure? If so, I'll give you a chance to put on some evidence.

MS. MAYFLOWER: No, Your Honor.

THE COURT: Mr. Keith, do you want to be heard further?

MR. KEYES: As to departure, no, Your Honor, I've mean there might be some comments but in light of the court's comments I don't know it's real necessary to make many comments in response to the government. I would just say that Mr. Farrell was pretty open about this. Him and other people were doing this down in Destin. The Coast Guard were aware of it.

Their main concern seemed to be inspecting the people to make sure they had things, that they weren't putting things damaging to the environment, but they weren't so interested in permits. He was open, way open about this. He wasn't trying to hide the fact he was doing this. So that makes me wonder what he believed his authority was to do that. But anyway, back in September, it seemed to come to a head in the summer of '93 where they really came down on him. He basically stopped doing it in September of '93 and yet this charge wasn't brought until two years later. And I say that in terms of the deterrent effect. It's not, you know, it was a long period between when he stopped doing this and when they actually charged him with doing this. It's part of the plea agreement in this case. But I agree with the court's comments, it's a confusing area. I tried to look into it more. I haven't had many cases myself in this environmental area and it's certainly not so crystal clear to me whether something sometimes violates a law, although I'm not arguing he didn't technically violate a law in this case that he pled to.

THE COURT: Again, the basic problem is the delegation problem. We have something being charged as a criminal offense which Congress has never said was a criminal offense. This particular conduct has never been addressed by Congress. It's only been made a criminal offense by interpretations and regulations and the Corps of Engineers and EPA and it's a grafted offense and by grafting it on to conduct that is normally subject to civil penalties then that's where I think there's a constitutional weakness. And I've said that before in other contexts. I think all of these environmental crimes have a very weak statutory underpinning and have a weak constitutional underpinning. But nevertheless, on the basis of where we are here, we've got a criminal offense which I'm prepared to go ahead and deal with on the facial application of the statute and the guidelines.

Under the application notes the application notes take into account that there are some factors that should and almost must be taken into account in the strict application of guideline 201.3. The base offense level here is three and if the offense resulted in an ongoing, continuous or repetitive discharge, release or emission of pollutant, increase by six levels, which has been applied here. 201.2(b)(4) says if the offense involved a discharge without a permit or in violation of a permit, increase by four levels, which once again has been applied here. The statutory definition of a pollutant once again is probably drafted by a legal intern because it's so wide and broad it encompasses every conceivable type of material that could be placed.

Title 33, Section 1462, says pollutant CV means dredge spoil, solid waste, incinerator residue, sewage, sewage sludge, chemical waste, radioactive materials, heat, but then we get very broad and general, wrecked or discarded equipment, rock, sand, cellar dirt, industrial, municipal and agricultural waste. Certainly, rock and sand apply to almost anything discharged into waters. But assuming that this is a pollutant for purposes of the application of 201.3 then the notes themselves in application note four to that guideline says subsection (b)(1) assumes a discharge or emission into the environment resulting in actual environmental contamination. Depending on the harm resulting from emission, release or discharge, the quantities and nature of substance of pollutant, duration and risk of violation, departure of up to two levels in either direction may be appropriate, and I find it is in this case downward and I make that downward departure two levels under application note four to the six-level enhancement under 201.3(b)(1).

Next, in application note seven it says subsection (b)(4) applies when the offense involved violation of a permit or whether there was failure to obtain permit when one was required, depending on the nature and quantity of the substance involved and risk associated with the offense departure of up to two levels in either direction may be warranted. Again, I find it is certainly in this case warranted as downward departure of two levels to the four-level increase that was previously applied. So, deducting the total of four levels from the offense level of thirteen results in a guideline offense level of nine for guideline purposes and criminal history category of one and a guideline range of four to ten months. Counsel, do you agree? Mr. Keyes?

MR. KEYES: Yes, Your Honor, I don't dispute that.

THE COURT: Ms. Mayflower, do you agree?

MS. MAYFLOWER: Yes, Your Honor.

THE COURT: So, with that, Mr. Keyes, would you like I to speak by way of allocution?

MR. KEYES: Well, we appreciate the court's decisions about the departures and reducing the guideline range. I had said in my letter that I thought in this particular case based on the overall circumstances and aim of the statute and some of the things the court had mentioned, it may be even a departure from the guideline might be appropriate to require some probation but not necessarily any custodial type of condition of home confinement. I know under these present guidelines, four to ten months, I guess the court would have to impose a minimum of four months of home detention or some other custodial condition. But we'd ask the court to consider a sentence of probation without any home detention being required. And I pointed out in the letter I submitted as to the reasons. I think this is a statute that's not really aimed at this kind of conduct, it's not the typical type of conduct that would be prosecuted under this statute and it's a circumstance that the commission did not consider in determining these guidelines.

THE COURT: I don't have your letter. Do you have it?

MR. KEYES: I had assumed it was attached to the report and I'm not sure, maybe it was not.

MS. MAYFLOWER: I've got a copy, Your Honor, if you would like to see it.

MR. KEYES: I've got the letter here. It would be the last paragraph.

THE COURT: Well, Mr. Keyes, what you have said is that Subchapter H, which has to do with ocean dumping, did not apply to placement of materials for the purpose of developing, maintaining or harvesting fishing resources. And does not apply to the construction of any fixed structure or artificial island or the intentional placement of any device in ocean waters, on or beneath submerged land beneath such waters when such construction is otherwise regulated by federal or state law or made pursuant to authorized federal or state program.

MR. KEYES: The point I was trying to make, Your Honor, is that I'm not arguing that he didn't violate the statute he pled guilty to. I'm not, you know, saying that, I mean as long as he didn't get the proper permit and authority for his reef building it appears that he would be violating this act possibly by not getting the proper permitting for that. But my point was the main purpose of the act that he's been charged with violating is it doesn't seem to be aimed at persons like him. I mean you have those exceptions that are noted in the regulations that seem to you say, well, if you act under proper authority we're really not saying ocean dumping means building artificial reefs or doing anything for a purpose other than disposal, you know. And I guess my point was I don't think the sentencing Commission in writing these guidelines as they have really had in mind someone like Mr. Farrell, who was building artificial reefs and trying to do so for purposes other than contaminating or polluting the waters and that type of thing.

THE COURT: Well, I think the people who put the guidelines together showed a remarkable understanding of some of the ramifications by allowing the departures.

MR. KEYES: Right.

THE COURT: I think the real problem is that the people that wrote the statute and enacted the statute didn't have any idea what they were encompassing by it. So, you're arguing for further departure? Is that what you're asking for?

MR. KEYES: As in my letter I was suggesting there could be a ground for further departure based on the commission not taking into account these particular circumstances of this statute.

THE COURT: Mr. Farrell, would you like to say anything personally?

THE DEFENDANT: No, sir, nothing, Your Honor.

THE COURT: Ms. Mayflower?

MS. MAYFLOWER: Your Honor, the Ocean Dumping Act includes criminal provisions for dumping pollutants into the ocean. I think that's a given. The court was very concerned about the fact--

THE COURT: Let me just give you an example. I was on a cruise ship three years ago and I watched them dump all the trash off the back of the ship in the ocean. Not just a bag or two but bags and bags and bags of it, which is perfectly legal. How come?

MS. MAYFLOWER: It's not perfectly legal, Your Honor, inside a particular zone within the waters of the United States. If they were to do something like that inside twelve miles, it's not perfectly legal. The problem we have is the jurisdictional problem once you get beyond that zone. You have jurisdictional problems whether you have jurisdiction over the ship's behavior. That's the problem. If they were to do something like that inside where we have jurisdiction it would definitely be a problem and prosecutable and in fact has been prosecuted at least down in Miami about three years ago. They prosecuted a cruise ship for doing just that very thing where a passenger of the cruise ship videotaped the behavior. They were able to prove it happened within the twelve miles where we had jurisdiction and they prosecuted the owners of the ship. It's a jurisdictional problem with that.

THE COURT: As long as they're outside twelve miles even though they're in the territorial fishing limits we have no jurisdiction to do that?

MS. MAYFLOWER: We have no jurisdiction, Your Honor, beyond our twelve-mile contiguous zone to exercise any kind of power over what the ship is doing. It's not a matter of Congress not thinking that that behavior is wrong.

THE COURT: All right.

MS. MAYFLOWER: The behavior is criminal.

THE COURT: I've got you off track and let me let you get back on. Go ahead.

MS. MAYFLOWER: Yes, Your Honor. My point is, Your Honor, you can say all day long you're building a reef but when you don't build the reef properly, when you use materials that are not conducive for reef building, when you build them indiscriminately, you go out every day and dump what amounts to garbage in the water day after day after day, you can call it reef building all day long but it's not. What it is dumping garbage. We're in a problem of semantics. We can call this reef building all day long. It's not. When you use improper materials and do it wrong and do it, so it harms the environment it's not building a reef. In fact, most of this material is not conducive to building reefs. It's not going to work. In two years, you're not going to have a reef there. All it has amounted to is dumping garbage into the ocean. And that's specifically what the Ocean Dumping Act prohibits criminally and that's what we have in this case.

THE COURT: What makes you say you won't have a reef there in two or three years?

MS. MAYFLOWER: Because, Your Honor, there are a lot of types of materials that reefs just won't grow on. You can put things out in the ocean, and they can sink to the bottom but that doesn't mean a reef is going to grow on that material. There are certain types of materials that are conducive for building of reefs and some types that are not, and you can put all the garbage you want to in the ocean but it doesn't mean a reef is going to grow there. And there are a lot of types of materials Mr. Farrell put in the ocean reefs will not build on.

THE COURT: What we're talking about here is steel.

MS. MAYFLOWER: Yes, Your Honor, and steel is traditionally, traditionally a conducive material for the building of reefs if it's done properly. If it moves around, if it's not anchored down, it will not be conducive to the growing of reefs. If it migrates at all, floats at all, reefs are not going to grow on it. That's why the Army Corps has specific regulations, because otherwise you're not building reefs; what you're going is dumping garbage. And that's what Mr. Farrell was doing and that's what takes his activity outside the realm of the Ocean Dumping Act. I also want to specify, Your Honor, that the court may find, and I, of course, as I said, respectfully disagree, but the court may find the statutory scheme in the environment law, particularly in the Ocean Dumping Act, is confusing with the regulations that apply to the Ocean Dumping Act. But specific to this case, Your Honor, it was not confusing because Mr. Farrell was told time and time and time again with letters, numerous letters exactly like the one I've attached to my letter to probation in response to Mr. Keye's letter, specifying specifically what Mr. Farrell himself had to do in order to get a permit and what he had to do to build a legal reef. In this case it was not confusing. He just refused to do it and he refused to do it for five or six years. We're not talking about something that happened once or twice and we're not talking about something he was confused about. And, yes, he was doing it out in the open, but he was doing it defiantly. He was doing it after the Coast Guard would tell him not to do it and he was lying continuously about whether he had a permit or not. His story would change every other day about whether he actually had a permit. He would lie and tell the coast Guard and other law enforcement he had a permit and he didn't. Specifically, in this case, Your Honor, the conduct, my point is that the conduct is egregious enough it's clearly within the Ocean Dumping Act in terms of the types of materials used and conduct of the particular defendant. And specific of this defendant, Your Honor, short of finding the statute unconstitutional the specifics in this case make the conduct a crime and make it egregious enough the departures the court has already granted to this defendant are more than enough, are extremely generous in reconciling the differences between this defendant's behavior and the behavior of a defendant who is, for example, pumping raw pollutants like sewage in the ocean. No further guideline departure is warranted or necessary in this case and I would submit that in terms of deterrent effect that that would be deleterious to our efforts to try to prevent these ocean dumpings from occurring in the future. That's all I have, Your Honor.

'Every day dumping garbage in the water? This woman is infected with something!' Matt thought to himself, he leaned over to Daniel and whispered, 'You need to say something!'

MR. KEYES: Your Honor, I just feel like, I know Mr. Farrell is probable chomping at the bit after hearing what Ms. Mayflower said because she said a lot of things and we probably disagree most strongly with almost all she said. I would point out a couple of things. Mr. Farrell was in the business of building reefs, People hired him to build reefs for them. And certainly, the material he would use for building the reef would have to be good reef building material or else he wouldn't be in the business very long if he just put things that were no good in the water. So, I mean he studied it, he knew what was good, and it's pretty common knowledge what would be good for building reefs and he used materials a lot of people are using to build reefs. And that was his purpose, it's a business, and also to help people to build reefs and the benefits that go along with reef building. So, I mean a lot of things we disagree with about saying he lied about this and did this and polluting every day, putting things in the water that are bad for the Gulf. That's not true and an exaggeration. I'm not going to get into more, but we disagree with a lot she said.

THE COURT: Well, let me simply say on the record I have been scuba diving many times on artificial reefs, certainly been fishing both private and commercial on artificial reefs, and I know artificial reefs attract and sustain and maintain the fishing populations. They attract and they serve a very important and useful function if done properly. And clearly those in the commercial fishing business or in the private fishing business like to establish them. So, they're desirable from many points of view. I don't think, certainly I don't think the statute is designed to really deal with that kind of activity, but it also is a regulated activity now which requires a permit. And once again, as I said when we started this proceeding, I think the real offense conduct here is that he was building artificial fishing reefs without a permit. Nevertheless, Mr. Farrell, I have reviewed your presentence report, and subject to the matters that have been corrected I find that it is accurate, and it's incorporated into your sentence as the law and sentencing procedure requires. Now pursuant to the sentencing Reform Act of 1984 and the sentencing guidelines it's the judgment of the court you're hereby sentenced to a term of probation for a period of two years in accordance with guideline 5C1.1(e) (3). This sentence is imposed within the sentencing guidelines and in accordance with the provisions of a guideline range B sentence, subject to a condition of home detention for four months which will be also subject to electronic monitoring which will be paid by you at your own expense. It's my determination based upon the financial information presented that you do not have the financial resources to pay a fine either within the range or below the range, so I'm waiving payment of a fine. But the law requires a monetary assessment of twenty-five dollars to be imposed in a class A misdemeanor, and it's so ordered. Your probation will be under the standard conditions of probation adopted by this court with the special condition as I've previously indicated of a period of home detention of four months to commence as soon as the probation officer can arrange for the monitoring to begin. I think that covers it. Mr. Law, anything else I need to include?

PROBATION OFFICER: He's got a special assessment. Your Honor, I'm not sure, is mandatory drug testing a blanket for all criminal proceedings?

THE COURT: No. All right under the Eleventh Circuit procedure do you have any objections to my findings or conclusions regarding Mr. Farrell's sentence? Anything from the defendant?

MR. KEYES: No, Your Honor.

MS. MAYFLOWER: No, Your Honor.

THE COURT: Let me advise you, you may appeal from a guideline sentence, Mr. Farrell, on grounds set out by statute in Title 18, United States Code, Section 3742. I believe that concludes everything with the sentencing. I don't know whose copy of the letter I got from Mr. Keyes and I also have one from the government so let me put them both to be made a part of the PSI. All right, We're in recess.

In light of the fact that Ms. Mayflower had pushed for $100,000 in fines and one year in jail Matt was ecstatic to pay the $25 dollars and take two years' probation. As far as the ankle monitor it was winter in Destin and long pants would cover that up. Leaving the courthouse Matt could not help but wonder what would have happened if he had fought back. But then his vision of Agent Ruby on a dark road, standing there with his gun drawn in front of a black crown Victoria came back to his mind and he grabbed Donna's hand and practically ran out of the Federal Courthouse.

# Chapter 13

*DESTIN, FLORIDA*

Ted and Mellie Hollis were in Destin for a long weekend. Ted had told Mellie they needed a break, but he wanted to check in with Brad and see what the status was on fishing in the gulf. They had invited Senator Alex Thibodaux to join them as they had a magnificent condo at Silver Shells with a stunning wrap around balcony overlooking the Gulf.

The threesome was headed down the Harbor to meet Brad for dinner.

At Marina Café' they were seated on a balcony overlooking the harbor. The senior senator ordered bottles of Kendall Jackson Chardonnay and a massive platter of fried crab claws to start the evening off right. The Senator had taken a quite a liking to Mellie and knew that for a political wife Ted could not have done better. Mellie was thrilled to have the Senator in their corner and this opportunity to get to know the elder statesman better.

The elder senator approved the wine and leaned over to pour Mellie a glass first. 'My dear you and Ted must tear yourselves away from Texas and Florida to come visit me in Washington.'

'Alex, we would love to! Perhaps you can arrange a Christmas White House tour for us?' Mellie smiled back.

Brad appeared at Ted's right hand and greeted the group. Handshakes and hugs went all around the table and another wine glass appeared. Brad ordered ceviche to go with the crab claws.

Brad reported to Ted and Alex that reef building in the Destin area had been curtailed by a strange prosecution of the Captain who had built most of the reefs and that the bag limits were being tightened in response to decreased fishing numbers. He did not ask why this made both men smile.

Down on the dock under the restaurant balcony Matt Ferrell was finishing the gel coat on a fiberglass repair on the Bottom Line.

The Captain told Matt that he had some very drunk tourists aboard fishing and when they pulled in a thrashing, bleeding, trying to bite everyone Mako shark rather than a huge grouper one of the drunk tourists had pulled a .38 pistol out of his fanny pack and started shooting. The ensuring chaos was made worse by his deckhand, Alfred Gibson, yelling 'Kamikaze!' and dive bombing the shooting tourist from the bridge, knocking his front teeth out on the deck as Alfred's huge body took him down. The captain reported to Matt that the gun went flying and no one found it and the tourist was madder about that then his missing teeth.

'Matt it has never crossed my mind to do bag searches when the tourists come aboard, but I'm thinking of changing that policy.'

Matt shook his head and laughed. Well you could not tell the Bottom Line had been full of .38 slugs now. It was good as new. He started to clean his rollers with acetone and gather his tools.

In the next slip, the Lucky Angler was coming in with a load. Matt looked up and saw that the tourists aboard were all on the back deck yelling and pointing at the wheelhouse, the deckhands were so nervous that one of them fell trying to grab the piling to tie up.

The tourists bailed before the other hand could put the gangplank down and continued pointing at the wheelhouse yelling. One was a woman and she pulled a cell phone out of her purse. Matt heard her say, 'dolphins, he shot them!', she gasped into the phone.

'This is not going to go good.' Matt thought, he gathered up the rest of his tools but decided to hang around to see what was going on.

The door to the wheelhouse banged open and the Captain leaned out with a fifth of Jack Daniels in his hand. 'Shut up you damn Yankees!' he yelled, 'you wanted fish you got fish!' He took a huge slug of the whiskey and slammed the door shut again.

One of the frightened deckhands took off running as two

Okaloosa Sheriff's deputies came up to the growing crowd that was getting louder by the minute.

Up on the restaurant balcony, Mellie said, 'what in the world is all that commotion down there?'

'Oh, it's probably some unlucky anglers.' Senator Thibodaux responded.

'whatever it is it does not concern us, we are here to relax and enjoy the fruits of our labor' Said Ted, casting a disinterested look over the balcony.

'hmmm...' Mellie contemplated the menu.

The waiter returned with two more bottles of wine and took orders. Platters of fried snapper, grilled stuffed snapper, blackened snapper and Red Snapper Livornese were ordered by the group.

Ted shoot one more look over the balcony and turned and picked up his wine glass, 'to the sunset over the harbor!' he said. Four wine glasses clinked together. 'yes, it's so beautiful, postcard perfect.' Mellie chimed in.

The sun was making its descent into the water and sky light up in brilliant orange with pink and lavender streaks woven in.

Down on the harbor the lights were blue as more police officers arrived on the scene.

Two deputies banged on the wheelhouse and the Captain opened the door. One grabbed his arm and asked him to please come down. The large older man complied and brought his Jack Daniels with him.

Matt was still watching the growing circus on the docks and recognized the Captain from the Harbor Coffee Shop. It was the Captain who had been complaining about the snapper regulations and the dolphins and spilled his coffee all over the bar. 'Oh man, what have you done?' Matt thought.

The Captain came down and disembarked his vessel to face the crowd. The crying woman who called the police started screaming, 'He shot the dolphins!' and started crying hysterically again.

'Look lady!' the captain said, 'your man was complaining that we could not catch a damn fish and he paid to take your ass fishing! We can't catch a fish because the one you did catch was not legal and when we throw it back it attracts the dolphin to a free meal like kids to an ice cream truck! All I did was run them off with a little lead poisoning so you could FISH. Cause that is what you people paid me to do!'

Matt stood frozen and staring in horror. This man just admitted to shooting at a protected marine mammal in front of a crowd of hostile witnesses and the cops. He was a goner...

The crowd gasped and the deputies were on the radio with dispatch trying to figure out what to do. Finally, the deputy who had escorted the Captain out of the wheelhouse pulled his handcuff's out.

The captain took another slug of the whiskey and yelled, 'to hell with the Marine Mammal Protections! To hell with all of you!' He kept yelling as the deputy handcuffed him and lead him away to the cheers of the crowd.

On the balcony, Brad had managed to convince Mellie to come fishing with the men in the morning. Mellie had had just enough wine to think this was a fine idea and even agreed to get up at four am to go along with them. 'Listen!' she said, 'The crowd is cheering the sunset! Isn't this fun?'

Matt stood there with his toolbox in one hand and a five-gallon bucket in the other, watching the Captain get escorted off the dock by the deputies.

He turned to the west and watched the sun slip below the horizon past the Destin Bridge. Taking a deep breath of salty ocean air, he thought, 'I wonder how Donna will feel about moving back to North Carolina?'

Matt walked away from the docks.

# Epilogue

'Ms. Bates? Phone for you. It's from Washington ma'am.'

Regina looked up from her messy mound of papers. 'Thank you.' She waved her hand to dismiss the intern then picked up the phone.

'This is Ms. Bates.' She snapped.

Regina listened and her eyes got wide.

'Why yes Senator, I'm sure I can help you with that. I was just reading some research on the benefits of a net ban you may find very interesting.' Her thin lips stretched into a smile.

# The Captain's Chapter

Many years have passed since the trial in Pensacola. Reef building out of Destin dwindled to a few fishermen occasionally hauling chicken coops, basically the only approved material for the private sector.

With artificial reef construction reduced so drastically the snapper, grouper, trigger and other species have nowhere to congregate. Without the spots to fish on the fisherman suffered in that the catch quotas dropped off to a point that many were forced financially into other professions.

With catch quota's showing reduced numbers of fish Regina Bates and the MFC implemented restrictive bag limits and seasons to catch certain species. Every time the MFC went before the politicians in Tallahassee things got worse and worse for the fisherman. Workshops were conducted in coastal communities in an attempt to find common ground between the fisherman and the powers that be. Fisherman would drive hundreds of miles to participate before the panels, pour out their hearts and plead for reasoning to spare their livelihood and way of life. At any one of these meetings the collective years of experience of the fisherman was in the hundreds if not thousands of years. Most members of the panels had never caught a fish in the Gulf of Mexico.

After months of these meetings where the fisherman had signed registers listing their years of experience and the name of their boats the MFC reps took the registers to Tallahassee to present them along with their own agenda of restrictions and bag limits and claim falsely that 'this is what the fisherman say we should do to preserve our resources in the Gulf.' The wisdom and advice from generations of fisherman was not regarded nor respected.

With the unrelenting restrictions on American Fisherman the unrestricted seafood from Mexico flowed in thanks to the North

American Trade Agreement. With this unlimited flow came an unlimited flow of profits for those in the know and set to profit.

With successful hook and line bag limits, the sights were set on nets.

Net fisherman with their miles of sophisticated nets were bringing in tons of fish to the American markets and this had to stop so imports could increase.

Net fishing has evolved over thousands of years of hard work. Fisherman have experimented with colors, weights, mesh size, floating buoys, float sizes, lengths and widths. A cast net is a circular net designed to be thrown into shallow water to catch bait fish or score a mullet for dinner.

An inshore gill net was usually carried on a shallow draft skiff in the bays and bayous. A fisherman would search for a school of mullet in five or six feet of water. Upon locating the school, he would throw a weight off of the stern and drive ahead allowing the weight to pull the net off the back of the boat. The idea is to encircle the school and drop the other end of the net to enclose the fish inside it. A float line would suspend the net like a curtain and the fish would swim into getting trapped in the net. The mesh was sized or designed to allow smaller fish to swim through only catching the bigger fish.

One of the most effective inshore nets was called a purse seine net. This net required a large boat and possibly a smaller take off boat. The fisherman would cruise along the shoreline in search of fish. Usually the target fish were cigar minnows, Boston mackerel, skipjack or ladyfish and herring. On sighting the school of target fish, the Captain would send the takeoff boat in one direction as he powered the boat around in another creating a circle around the school. The float line suspended the top of the net as lead rings pulled the bottom downward. Once the two ends were brought together a line threaded through the rings was pulled tight closing the bottom like a lady's purse. A crew of about 4 guys would dip the fish out of the net into a hold in the vessel. A good strike could net up to forty thousand pounds of fish.

The menace of the fishing industry was the offshore gill net. The Japanese had perfected a way to kill everything. The offshore gill net was so destructive that American fisherman refused to use them.

It had been designed to catch the high dollar and highly prized yellow fin and bluefin tuna along with swordfish. These fish are swimming gold in Japan and America. The mesh design of the offshore gill net was large openings with a fine mesh design so the fish's sonar could not detect the net. Thus, the fish would swim into the nets and become entangled and die. Large sharks would become entangled trying to eat the fish already in the net...

Huge ships would stretch miles of these nets across the oceans. Turtles, tuna, sharks, swordfish, marlin, dolphins, wahoo, sailfish, whales and even Flipper the Friendly porpoise would meet their fate in this curtain of death.

The NAFTA pirates got busy. Adding a 'Net Ban' to the Fishing Enhancement Act would stop all forms of net fishing and cripple the American fishing industry. With the November elections only a few months away the propaganda machine was fired up full speed ahead. All it took was showing a video of Flipper, God's smiling hero of the oceans trapped and entangled in a net on the evening news. Children would have nightmares of Flipper, smiling, even though dead in a net to enrage mother's all over America. It got so bad, people marched in the streets demanding the heads of these monster fisherman who strangled to death the precious smiling angel of the Oceans. 94% of the country voted to 'ban the nets'.

Now a method of fishing documented even in the Bible was now banned. And the skyrocketing demand for seafood was met with fish caught in other waters and imported to our country.

The net ban affected all nets and all forms of net fishing, not just the dastardly offshore gill net. It even affected the guy throwing his cast net off a dock. The only nets not affected by the new law were shrimp nets. Shrimpers had learned that politicians were a good investment.

With the banning of gill nets in the bays and bayou's the mullet have multiplied to the point where many die from oxygen depletion in the waters.

The banning of purse seine nets affected hundreds of hardworking fishermen in every coastal community. The amount of fish these fishermen used to catch has grown to a point where millions of fish are dying along the shoreline. All these dead fish have attracted sharks to come in close to the beaches to feast without limits. In turn the number of shark attacks on swimmers has greatly increased over the past decade with many more to come.

The devastation on the turtle population has become drastic. The sharks view baby turtles as fresh Krispy Kreme donuts and the 'Hot Light' is on for the sharks during hatching season.

Because of the restrictions on snapper the Gulf is full of them. About five months ago I was speaking with an FWC Officer that had just gone fishing on a charter boat out of Destin. He told me that on this trip he threw back sixty snappers. This particular charter boat is called a 'party boat' which means it carries up to fifty fisherman per trip. With this many hooks in the water, thousands of snappers are caught and thrown back and the porpoises love eating them. The porpoises (dolphins) follow the boats from spot to spot to gorge themselves on disoriented snappers.

After fifteen years of this, the dolphin, once regarded as the most proficient hunter in the water is now the most annoying beggar. Once a boat stops to fish on a spot the dolphin show up. The captain may choose to move on to another spot to get away from the dolphins, but they will follow and tell their buddies so now it's six dolphins stripping the hooks.

The fisherman hate the dolphins to the point where one captain told me they killed thirty-four dolphins in one day. 'we shot them till we ran out of bullets...' his words, not mine.

The Marine Mammal Protection Act of 1972 states, 'it shall be considered illegal to feed a dolphin in the wild. Behavior of wild marine mammals' changes when humans feed them. Normally shy and timid animals learn to seek out humans for food. There is evidence that dolphins learn to steal from fishing lines, after learning to receive food from people. This brings the mammals into close proximity to fishing vessels endangering their lives.'

Very few people have profited off of the North American Trade Agreement and many have suffered. The total devastation on the fisheries in the Gulf of Mexico has yet to be seen. The greed of a few people has altered the course of nature. In fifty years when the scientific evidence and research reveals what has happened in the Gulf people will scratch their heads and say, 'all this from a few crooked politicians and a ridiculous Bag Limit....'

Captain Steven F. Gilbert
Destin, Florida

# About the Authors

Captain Steven F. Gilbert has been a resident of Destin for over 35 years. He loves the Gulf of Mexico, boats, and fine seafood. In another time, Steve would have been welcomed as a traveling raconteur as there is nothing, he loves more than telling a good story. You can find him on a houseboat somewhere along the Gulf of Mexico

Alana Haase is a non-fiction author and a nurse of 30 years. Bag Limit is her first work of fiction with more to come as there is nothing she loves as much as reading or writing a good story.


You can reach the author through Alana's website at www.AlanaKHaase.com and subscribe to the email list there.

# If you enjoyed this book, will you consider sharing it with others?

Amazon reviews are very important to independent authors, please leave a review if purchase of this book was made on Amazon.

You can also follow Alana's author page on Amazon.

Mention this book on Facebook, Twitter or a blog post! Gift a copy of this book to a friend who would enjoy a good fish tale!

We thank you for your support and hope you enjoyed Bag Limit!

www.ingramcontent.com/pod-product-compliance
Lightning Source LLC
Chambersburg PA
CBHW030750110726
47900CB00008B/2542